THE HORRORS
Terrifying Tales

Book One

THE HORRORS
Terrifying Tales

Book One

Edited by Peter Carver

Red Deer PRESS

PUBLISHED BY
Red Deer Press
813 MacKimmie Library Tower
2500 University Drive N.W.
Calgary Alberta Canada T2N 1N4
www.reddeerpress.com

CREDITS
Edited for the Press by Peter Carver
Copyedited by Jane Grove
Cover design & illustration by Peter Ledwon & Marilyn Mets
Text design by Erin Woodward
Printed and bound in Canada by Friesens for Red Deer Press

ACKNOWLEDGMENTS
Financial support provided by the Canada Council, the Government of Canada through the Book Publishing Industry Development Program (BPIDP), and the Alberta Foundation for the Arts, a beneficiary of the Lottery Fund of the Government of Alberta.

THE CANADA COUNCIL | LE CONSEIL DES ARTS
FOR THE ARTS | DU CANADA
SINCE 1957 | DEPUIS 1957

NATIONAL LIBRARY OF CANADA CATALOGUING IN PUBLICATION
Carver, Peter, 1936–
The horrors : terrifying tales / Peter Carver.
ISBN 0-88995-313-9 (v. 1)
1. Horror tales, Canadian (English) I. Title.
PS8605.A775H67 2005   jC813'.6   C2005-902477-1

3 9082 10310 7010

Contents

Introduction

Ever wonder who the bogeyman really was?

Or what happens inside those family vaults in the cemetery at night?

What do you do when you know you're about to die? Or realize you're already dead?

In *Horrors I,* some of Canada's finest writers for young people (some well known to you, others less familiar) delve into the dark corners of their imaginations, exploring the creepy, disturbing possibilities that haunt the human soul. Within these pages is that visit from the bogeyman. There are werewolves. A pale, drowning figure appears under the river ice. Some of the scariest images in these stories are those that give macabre twists to everyday life and events: the tortured death of an innocent high school student, the recovered memory of a grinning, murderous stepfather. With the possible exception of the evoking of the ghost of Johnny Cash, none of these is a particularly hopeful tale.

Dennis Johnson's suggestion that we gather a collection of horror stories did not, at first, meet with the wholesale endorsement of his overly purist children's editor. For one thing, I thought, weren't horror stories a kind of inferior cultural artifact? Then I thought of Ray Bradbury's shivery little masterpiece, "The Small Assassin" (not recommended for mothers-to-be), and the perennial appeal in W.W. Jacobs's "The Monkey's Paw," not to mention Saki's "The Open Window." And the marvelously composed Conrad Aiken story, "Mr. Arcularis," that has haunted me since I first heard the CBC's dramatic radio version starring John Drainie. To say nothing of Edgar Allen Poe's darkly melodramatic "The Gold Bug" read aloud in an elementary classroom one rainy Friday afternoon.

So the purist wavered, put out tentative feelers to the community of writers for children and young adults in Canada. There were some who fended off the request, saying, "I don't want to visit that country; it's too close, too scary. But for the most part the responses were enthusiastic. (Writers apparently like to scare themselves sometimes, the way many readers do.)

Before long I was snowed under by all manner of original, never-before-published, "horrible stories" (as one writer jokingly expressed it) and soon realized we had enough quality stuff for two anthologies rather than one. We seemed to have struck a receptive note among creative people who we always thought were quite nice but who obviously had darker and more sinister undercurrents flowing through their imagination.

The enthusiasm of the authors may have arisen from the opportunity to work on plots that don't end so happily after all. Writers for young people have engraved on their conscience a sense of duty to make sure their protagonists emerge triumphant, morally or otherwise, at the end of the story. But horror stories, by definition, don't carry that requirement. Horror stories visit the depths and sometimes lodge there—fixed in nightmare country where there is always a chance of snakes, where phobias come true, and where you need to watch what you eat and which dark rooms you enter.

Each of these stories illuminates a distinct path through fearful territory—for readers fourteen to forty and beyond who thrive on the stimulation of a chilling tale. Enjoy them if you can. If you must.

Peter Carver
Everton, June 2004

PULL

Don Aker

Adam was four when he first saw them. He was holding Gramma's hand as the two stood waiting for the Walk sign on Oakland Avenue. Or, more accurately, she was holding *his* hand, keeping him from darting in front of traffic. They'd just emerged from the subway on their way to Waverley Zoo, and he'd been wound drum-tight with excitement ever since she'd told him where they were going.

The sudden bright after the gloom of the transit tunnel had made his eyes water, so he didn't see them at first. But even behind his tears, he could feel them. A pull. Like the way his skin puckered out when he put his hand over the nozzle of the vacuum, the suction tugging at him, drawing him in.

Wiping the wet from his eyes with his free hand, Adam saw them standing on the opposite side of the street. Waiting. But not like the others who stood watching the picture of the red hand above Adam's head. They were waiting for something else. Adam knew because they weren't looking at the hand. They were looking at the two people on the curb in front of them: a woman and a man. The woman was dressed in a suit and held a briefcase like the one Adam's father carried with him to work. The man beside her was dressed in shorts and a T-shirt, both dark with sweat. He wore headphones and he jogged on the spot, his sneakered feet keeping time with music that Adam couldn't hear.

"Look, Gramma," said Adam. He pointed at the two figures behind the woman and the man.

"I see," said Gramma.

But Adam knew she didn't. She thought he was pointing at the sign across the street, the one with the picture of the lion on it beside the words Zoo Ahead. She knew he could read "Zoo" because he always pointed to it in the book she'd given him last week when she'd come to visit. *Zack Goes to the Zoo* was now his favorite. Even better than *The Cat in the Hat*.

But that wasn't what he meant. "No," he said. "There." He pointed again at the two figures. "The eels." He felt the pull again and he suddenly shivered in the August sunshine.

"Eels?" asked Gramma, looking at him with raised eyebrows.

Of course, they *weren't* eels, but he had no other words for them. His father had taken him fishing earlier that summer when they'd gone to his uncle's cottage for the weekend. It was his first time in a boat, and his father had just been telling him how people never caught anything their first time out when Adam's small, blue rod had bent nearly double. He remembered how the buckles on his life jacket had tightened as he shrieked with delight, making him feel like a balloon about to burst. That is, until his father had helped him reel in his fish.

The eel smashed the water when it surfaced, twisting furiously around the line, looping over itself in the air as his father swung it into the boat. Adam had shrieked again but this time in fear, and even his father had drawn back when it slapped the fiberglass bottom. Adam scrambled away from the creature writhing at his feet, tying and untying itself like wet ribbon, and he'd begged his father to toss it back. Grim-faced, his father had gripped the coiling body and tried to remove the hook, but the eel had swallowed it whole. He reached behind him for the dip net, held its metal handle like a hammer as he whacked the creature with it. Once. Twice. The eel stopped squirming, and his father cut the line with his jackknife and tossed it overboard. It was only when the creature was gone that Adam crept close to his father, crawled into the safety of his big arms.

Adam remembered the feeling of that rod in his hands, the sudden pull that drew it downwards. He felt that same pull now as he pointed to the figures across the street that stood motionless behind the woman and the man.

Motionless until now.

At exactly the same moment, they raised their hands and placed them on the shoulders of the woman with the briefcase and the man with the headphones. Neither seemed to notice. Instead, they stepped off the curb and into the crosswalk, heading toward Adam and his grandmother. But Adam and his grandmother didn't move, even though the red hand had become a green man. Instead, they watched an oncoming car swerve suddenly out of control, careening toward the crosswalk and the woman and the man. Gramma called out, but it was too late.

Adam still remembered the sounds of their bodies hitting the pavement. It was the same sound the metal handle of the dip net had made when it struck the eel. Wet and final.

$$\times \ \times \ \times \ \times \ \times$$

Adam stood outside the biology lab waiting for Erin. As usual, she would be the last to leave. He peered over the heads of the other students streaming from the room, saw her talking to the teacher, pointing to something under a microscope as she absently brushed a lock of yellow hair from her face. The teacher bent toward the microscope, looked through the lens, then straightened and said something in return. Erin grinned and Adam felt a familiar wedge of emotion move through his chest. Her smile always did that to him, crowded out everything else, took his breath away. She'd laughed when he told her that once, accused him of watching too many reality shows where strangers fell in love with strangers between commercials.

But she was no stranger. He'd known her all his life. The fact that they'd met only last term when she'd transferred to Winslow High was a mere technicality. It was like they fit somehow. He'd felt it the moment he saw her across the cafeteria, felt his stomach bottom out and his heart hammer against his rib cage.

Of course, getting *her* to realize they belonged together hadn't been easy.

She'd hated him on the spot.

Well, maybe she didn't hate him, but he was everything she wasn't looking for. "Hockey player," she'd said when she'd turned toward his "Hi" and saw the lettering on his jacket. "I don't like hockey."

Adam had stood clutching his cafeteria tray, groping for more words. He'd never had trouble talking to girls before. He was one of the most aggressive forwards on the Winslow Warriors, but off the ice he had a cool and easy manner that drew people to him, girls in particular. He was used to *them* starting conversations with *him*. His face flaming, he'd opened his mouth to say something else, anything else. But she'd already turned and moved off through the crowd.

Erin picked up her biology books and turned toward the door, saw Adam, and smiled at him through the other stragglers. The wedge came again, and he fought the urge to push past the remaining students and kiss her. He thought of the first time they'd kissed, the evening she'd finally agreed to go out with him after a dozen curt refusals. "You're worse than a stalker," she'd frowned when he cornered her in the library with two tickets to the Whiteblade concert. But she went with him, and that had been their beginning.

"Hey, Adam."

Adam turned to see Connor McAllister, the tall redhead who played defense for the Warriors. "Connor," he said, pointing to his team-mate's sling. "How's the shoulder?"

"Dislocated. Doc says I gotta sit out the next week." Connor shook his head sadly. "No triple A tournament for me."

"Tough break," said Adam. He felt a tug and glanced over his shoulder to see if Erin had come out, and he froze.

His mind registered that Connor was still talking, sharing details of the car accident that had sidelined him, embellishing the story he'd probably told a dozen times already that day, but Adam heard none of it. All he could hear was the sudden rush of blood in his ears and the moan that came from deep inside him. Erin was nearly at the doorway of the lab, laughing at something Carla Peterson had just told her. Immediately behind her stood an eel.

X X X X X

"And nobody else sees them?" asked Erin. She sat beside him on the bench at the bus stop, and her breath made quick exclamation points in the February air. A bus had already come and gone, but neither she nor Adam had noticed.

Adam shrugged. He was shivering, but not because of the cold. He was trying not to panic, trying not to give in to the fear he thought he'd put behind him. He hadn't intended to tell her. But she'd known immediately that something was wrong, could see it in his eyes, read it in the lines on his face. Could hear it in his voice as he'd greeted her, grasped her hand, and led her quickly outside. She'd begged him to tell her what was suddenly so wrong.

He'd told her about the first time, that day with his grandmother near Waverley Zoo. And about some of the times after that. On the school playground in grade two, just before Kaleigh Philips had fallen from the jungle gym and broken her neck. The Thanksgiving morning his grandmother had had the stroke that killed her. The day in junior high before his math teacher, Mr. Leighton, had gone home and flicked on his kitchen light, igniting the propane explosion that obliterated him and two friends.

He'd told her that the "when" was never the same. And it was never as immediate as that first time. Sometimes it was hours; sometimes days. Like his neighbor, Mrs. Rivers, who had an eel follow her to the end of her driveway on garbage day. She'd been rolling out her green compost bin, unaware of the ghost-like hand that found her shoulder as she positioned the bin at the curb. It was two days later that she slipped in her bathroom, and a full day after that when someone finally found her.

He didn't tell her everything. He didn't tell her about the countless times he'd seen the eels on buses, at movie theatres, in shopping malls, at McDonald's. What was the point? He hadn't known the people they stood behind. He only knew what happened to them. Eventually.

He told her about the therapists, though. The doctors his parents had taken him to see when, as a four-year-old, he couldn't explain why he was suddenly so afraid. He'd tried to tell them, but even then he knew they didn't understand, would never understand. At first, his talk of eels was the result of the trauma he experienced at witnessing the accident. When it continued, it was separation anxiety, dissociative disorder, a dozen other ailments and syndromes. Never "illness," though, and never "disease." Just growing pains a kid needed to work out.

And friends were no better. The few he'd told had laughed, kidded him about watching too many late-night thrillers. Even Kyle, his best friend since fifth grade, had looked at him like he'd suddenly grown two heads.

So he'd stopped talking about the things he saw. Turned a blind eye to his knowledge of the inevitable. And somehow it became easier. After Gramma, it was mostly people he didn't really know anyway. And sports helped. Soccer and hockey, especially. As the years passed, he found if he kept himself active, pushed his body to the limit, wore himself out, he didn't see the eels. Not as many, anyway. And when he was exhausted, it was easier to pretend not to see the ones he did.

But now there was Erin.

"No," he said softly. "Nobody else sees them."

She looked across the busy street, her eyes focused on some point outside herself, but he knew she was trying to keep from turning around, looking behind her. "But you're *sure* they're there?"

Surprisingly, there was no doubt in her voice, just a need for affirmation, and he was reminded of the feeling he'd had when he first saw her, how they fit together, like they were pieces of the same puzzle. He squeezed her hand, both fearful and grateful for her trust. "Not now," he said. There had been no eels since they'd left the school. He'd glanced behind them repeatedly, but each time he knew he'd see nothing. There had been no pull.

He felt her tremble, heard her draw a long, shuddering breath. She turned to him, her face an ashen mask, and he watched her force a thin smile. "Then everything's okay?"

He drew her close, folded his arms around her. Tried not to let her feel his fear.

X X X X X

"You're sure about this?" she asked.

Adam was sure of nothing. But if he could keep them from touching her, putting their hands on her, maybe he could stop it, somehow keep it from happening. It was a chance, anyway.

They had ridden the bus to the downtown terminal and switched to the subway, crisscrossing the city on the blue line and then the red. They'd stopped only once to withdraw some cash from a bank machine, using it to buy a bag full of tokens, plus some coffee and chocolate bars—the caffeine they needed to stay awake. Taking his bank card from the slot, Adam imagined the beginnings of a pull and he took Erin's hand and hurried her back onto the train, looking back only when they left the platform. But he saw nothing.

"I'm sure," he lied. "We can cheat them. I can tell when they're close. We just have to keep moving."

And they did. Afternoon stretched into evening and they continued to ride. Erin had already called her parents on her cell, told them some story about a missed deadline for a history project and having to work all night with her friend, Julia. Adam was surprised they'd believed her. Erin never missed deadlines. But, then again, she never lied.

He'd called his own parents too, and they'd accepted his similar story. They never worried about him like they did his sister, Jen, who got the third degree whenever she was five minutes late. He was, after all, a Winslow Warrior.

Making that call, Adam had felt almost normal. Felt like a guy conspiring to spend all night with the girl he loved. For a moment, he wasn't fleeing, wasn't trying to outrun something that no one else could see. But then the moment passed and the fear was on him again, its taloned fingers clawing at the base of his spine, scrabbling up his back, and sinking into the soft flesh of his neck. He pulled Erin close to him, breathed in the scent of her hair, felt her skin moist and warm against his. Held her tight.

Sometime during the night, despite the caffeine, he dozed off. He was climbing those subway stairs again with his grandmother, putting up his hand to block the sudden sun, still excited about the zoo. His grandmother was holding his other hand, her fingers entwined in his. Oddly, she was singing, her voice high and thin. But then he knew she wasn't singing. She was screaming. As bodies made wet and final sounds against pavement.

He woke with a jolt and his sudden movement startled Erin, nestled against him.

"Wha—" she began, but he placed a finger on her lips.

"It's nothing," he murmured. "Just a dream." He looked down at her face, alternately dark and light as the subway train sped between fluorescent tubes along the tunnel. For the thousandth time he marveled at how pretty she was. The dusting of freckles on her nose, the tiny white line in her eyebrow where she'd gotten stitches after falling from a bike, the spackle of brown in her otherwise startlingly blue eyes—all these imperfections only served to make her more beautiful. He bent toward her and kissed her, tasting chocolate and coffee and something else that was indefinably Erin.

Then he felt the pull.

He jerked his head upward, saw there was no one in front of them in the subway car. He looked back, and a sob tore at his throat.

"What's wrong?" Erin whispered, clutching at him. "What do you see?"

There were three people sitting behind them. A thin woman with a ripped parka, boots too big for her, a huge cloth bag in her lap. An elderly Chinese man with a felt hat and a red scarf wrapped several times around his neck. A man in his twenties, his spiked blue hair and pierced lips a vivid contrast to the London Fog overcoat he wore. And behind each of them was an eel.

But this wasn't what had turned Adam's veins to ice, his legs to liquid.

Eels sat behind both Erin and him.

Beneath him, Adam felt the wheels of the subway train lock, heard them shriek against the rails. Smelled the friction in the air, tasted it like burnt toast in his mouth. Saw in his darkening mind's eye the stalled car on the track immediately ahead. But he was aware of only one thing. The hand on his shoulder, pulling.

X X X X X

Born in Windsor, Nova Scotia, Don Aker began writing in 1988. His first short story, "The Invitation," won the 1989 Atlantic Writing Competition, was short listed for McClelland & Stewart's Journey Prize Award *for best short fiction published in Canada in 1990, and earned him a $10,000 grant from Telefilm Canada to assist him in adapting it to a feature-length screenplay, which won the Atlantic Film Festival's 1998 Script Development Competition. His story "The Test" won Canadian Living Magazine's 1990 National Literary Competition for best short fiction, his story "Scars" was a winner in Dandelion Magazine's 1991 Short Fiction Competition, and his story "Everything Gets Dead" was chosen runner-up in the Toronto Star's 2002 Short Story Contest. A junior high teacher, Don has also published several educational texts and three young adult novels:* Of Things Not Seen *(winner of the 1996 Ann Connor Brimer Award and 1996 Canadian Authors' Association Lilla Stirling Award),* Stranger at Bay, *and* The First Stone. *HarperCollins will publish his fourth YA novel,* One on One, *in 2005. Don lives in Middleton, Nova Scotia, with his wife and two daughters.*

THE BOY WRITING

Brian Doyle

The boy writes his assignment for school. He is writing well. He knows that what he writes is right: he can feel it down his back. He sits at the shaky, green table with the loose leg. His back is to the open door of the little room. His little room at home.

If the boy looks up from his work, he sees his reflection in the tear-stained window in front of him.

He writes well about a father who abuses his son. About the father's explosions of anger and hate.

He's at the part where the father is sitting with the boy's teacher. They are discussing the boy's F in English.

"I'm afraid he's missed so many assignments," the teacher says.

The father feels the skin tighten on his temples.

"However," says the teacher, "what little he did hand in was outstanding, very moving in fact. Very disturbing, even. 'Specially on the subject of the family."

The father feels something in the teacher's eyes, something unsaid, something accusing. He wants to drive his massive fist into the teacher's face. Wipe that look away.

Out in the parking lot, he wishes he'd demanded to see this essay or story or whatever the fuck did they call it nowadays, take it home, confront the boy with it, what is this garbage you write about your family, anyway?

The father scrapes the ice off the windows of his car. There's rage in the thrusts he makes with the scraper. He wants to cut the scraper into the glass itself.

The boy describes the scream of the smoking tires as the father spins his wheels through ice to asphalt.

The father goes to the tavern and laughs with his friends there and drinks beer.

The boy describes in his writing assignment how popular the father is at the tavern. How witty he is. How he sets the table roaring. How jolly.

The boy is writing well about how jolly.

He can feel it down his back.

Now the father drives dangerously home.

He wonders what things the boy could be writing about. Family things that are nobody's business. Nobody's. And that's not the first time, no. Told the school nurse that time that I burned him with a cigarette. Because he cut the page out of our encyclopedia for his project. How's somebody else supposed to use the encyclopedia if all the fucking pages are ripped out of it? Can you tell me that? Look at me! Can you tell me that?

The father pulls into his laneway and surprisingly doesn't slam the car door. He eases it shut, quietly clicking. He treads carefully on the frozen, wooden veranda steps, hoping they won't crack and pop with his weight.

The boy writes well about the sound the veranda doesn't make. The father eases his key into the lock and slides into the house in winter silence.

He drapes his coat over the banister. The boy describes the father's coat. The terrifying feel of the fabric. Then, like a ghost, the father moves down into the cellar.

Behind the stairs he feels for the plastic baseball bat.

The boy, in his writing, describes the bat: the feel of it, the sting of it.

Back on the first floor now. The father removes his shoes and, with one hand along the silky banister, goes up, taking the mute stairs two at a time.

He passes his wife's bedroom with the heavy, shut door. Now he stands hunched in the carpeted hallway, in the yellow light spilling from the open door of the little room.

He sees the boy there. Writing.

The father carries the bat against his leg and moves into the room, reaching for the boy's hair with his free hand.

The boy looks up from the shaky, green card table and sees both their reflections in the tear-stained window.

His pen is poised.

X X X X X

Brian Doyle is one of Canada's best-loved children's authors. His award-winning books have been published internationally and have been made into films and plays.

It was as a young boy, growing up in the Gatineau Hills north of Ottawa, that he picked up his love of stories and anecdotes. His teen memories of childhood—the settings, the people, the atmosphere, the special rhythm and ring of the local language—figure prominently in his eleven novels.

He also experiments, at times, with different formats—as in "The Boy Writing."

Brian's latest novel, Boy O'Boy, won the 2004 Canadian Library Association Book of the Year Award

and the 2004 Ruth Schwartz Award. He is the 2005
winner of the $25,000 NSK Neustadt Prize for
Children's Literature.

INVISIBLE TO DOGS

R.P. MacIntyre

"He's innocent. He wouldn't do that. You don't have no proof." Carl whined like a chainsaw. But it was clear they were both guilty as sin, him and his dog. You don't wear a look like that if you're innocent, that pee-pool-on-the-floor look. No, you don't do that. That'll get you nowhere. It never does. Bodies are strewn across the entire planet, their life's blood settled like blue lead in a bag, and no one says they did it. No one claims responsibility.

Still, it was nice to see him take a stand. Carl usually just let people think whatever they wanted. And people, being people, always thought the worst, and they were usually right. So it was hard to imagine why he should make such a claim this time. But if his dog didn't do it, who did? I don't even want to go there.

The last time Carl got caught for something, it was for stealing a truck. He was still in it, so that made things a little simpler. Carl liked things to be simple and needed them that way too. The shortest distance between two points is a straight line, and Carl was not one to go looking for curves. You want something? Take it. You don't want something? Throw it away.

Carl didn't like his name too much—too many curves in it. The sound alone had a curve in it, not to mention the half-looped C. He would have preferred something straighter—Stan, say, or Joe, like his uncle. In grade school, Carl had tried to get people to call him Ike for a while, like the American president, but it didn't catch on. There was no reason to call him Ike, other than Carl telling you to, and no one ever listened to Carl. Which was fair enough because Carl never listened to anyone either—certainly not his mom, and he didn't have a dad. Kids like Carl never do.

Carl was two grades behind, so he quit school and got a job at Manny's Muffler, Battery, and Brakes. Then he moved out of his mom's basement and got a dog. He called the dog Ike. The dog was as dumb as a post, which is to say it was slightly smarter than Carl. He would take off at night and chase cars or trucks. Unlike most dogs, Ike knew what to do when he caught one. He'd follow the vehicle till it stopped, then attack the driver as he (or she) was getting out. He'd go for their feet.

The amazing thing was that Ike was blind. He had eyes the color of half-boiled egg whites.

It took awhile to figure out just whose dog was doing this and identify it, but when I finally did and notified Carl that I was coming to destroy Ike, he said he'd do it himself. And to prove he did it, he came into the office and plunked the dog's carcass on my desk, minus the eyes. "Ravens got 'em," Carl said. It was a messy kill. His jaw was shot off and a fair amount of his blood wrecked half of last month's traffic reports, not that anyone reads them anyway. When they dried, I filed them like they were. The Ike reports.

I suppose the reason Carl liked the name Ike, aside from it being straight and short, is because he thought it was presidential. Presidents had power, and Carl had none. Maybe he thought some of that power came with the name. Carl couldn't have remembered that Ike's last name was Eisenhower, a name as curvy as Maryanne

Ravenhurst, the girl found lying on the road just north of here by someone walking their dog. She was more dead than alive, like that victim last year mauled by a bear, except she didn't get buried and it wasn't her head chewed off.

X X X X X

Some people are afraid or brave, like some people are tall or short, or have other distinctive characteristics. Like Carl Danziger has four toes. And I am invisible to dogs. Which is very handy because I love running and my normal route takes me down Churchill Drive past a zillion dogs, out onto the lake trail north of town, cluttered with hardy outdoorsy types exercising their canines. It doesn't bother me if they're not leashed.

The only thing that makes me feel vaguely uncomfortable is being ogled. I hate it when people stare at me. It gives me the heebie-jeebies. Especially when creeps like Carl Danziger do it. I can feel his eyes crawl on me like baby mice. Ever since grade three when he would follow me home from school, thinking I couldn't see him. But I could. Just like that time I saw his four-toed foot when his socks came off in his too-big boots, and he hurried to put them back on. I'm grateful he dropped out of school a couple of years ago and no longer lurks in the hallways, limping from locker to locker.

Since this is a northern town, it is filled with dogs and ravens. The dogs come in two sizes: large and extra-large; the ravens, just one: jumbo. For their morning snacks, ravens pluck small dogs from front yards. If the small dogs should survive the ravens, the coyotes get them. For their safety, small dogs must be locked indoors, 24/7. There they'll just become neurotic and bug-eyed, but they'll live. Cats, on the other hand, seem to have a knack for surviving these "natural" disasters, but too often wind up as furry little speed bumps on the side of the road, blood oozing from their meowless mouths, victims of passing delivery trucks.

Cats are blind to trucks, just like dogs are blind to me—except I don't go running *over* dogs. I run *by* them.

I realized at an early age that I was invisible to dogs. My sister, Beatta, was / is the opposite: not only is she visible to dogs, it seems they can see nothing else. She still carries two small scars where our neighbor's terrier escaped from their house, leaped *over* me, and seized Beatta by the nose.

There it was, this stupid little dog hanging from her face while she screamed, flapping her arms like she was trying to fly from the scene.

I took one swing at the dog and sent him skittering onto his butt. He scrambled to his feet and looked up at me as if to say, *Where the hell did you come from?* Then he took off like a shot. A raven had landed nearby.

Beatta held her nose while blood streamed between her fingers. "What did you do that for?" she screamed and tried to kick me with her boots.

I didn't understand what she meant, but Beatta holds it against me still, like I was somehow responsible for the scars on her nose. Maybe I was. I never told her about how that was the first time I realized I was invisible to dogs.

Then began my invisible encounters with dogs, like fights my friends would get me to break up. With three or four dogs tearing into one other, someone would yell, "Maryanne, stop them!" and I would dutifully enter the fray but never actually succeed. Sometimes they would stop of their own accord, but it gave my friends some kind of kick to see a person so close to danger but unharmed by it—sort of like a fire walker not getting burned.

There were also the neighbors with the wolf-dog. It had yellow eyes and a snarl that sounded like it was gurgling blood. It ripped into anyone who passed through their gates. The wolf-dog neighbors thought this fair enough because they posted two big Beware of Dog signs as ample warning. If you couldn't read or thought it was a bluff, too bad for you. I, however, regularly climbed their back yard fence to retrieve balls and Frisbees. The dog never lifted an eyebrow.

One day, an RCMP constable came to the wolf-dog neighbor's house. Constable Denis. I watched him unsnap his holster and pull out his gun before he opened the gate. He entered. First I heard the blood-gurgling snarl, then four gunshots and three yelps—each shot followed by a yelp except the last. The shots sounded like firecrackers, but sharper and more contained—little packages of death. I guess that's what bullets are.

Pellets from pellet guns are not quite packages of death—just packages of maiming and pain. I know because, at my sister's prodding, I've fired them myself. Beatta has one of those guns and takes delight in firing rounds of pellets into the hides of passing critters, furred or feathered. I'm not a good shot, but I hit a dog once—in the eye.

One day we were walking to school when two dogs appeared from behind some bushes. They were nearly full-grown German shepherds minding their own business or minding whatever dogs mind around bushes. However, Beatta threw a rock at them. Why she threw the rock, I can only guess, but they turned, bared their fangs and in about three bounds were on top of her, knocking me over on their way. One had hold of her leg and the other, her arm. Beatta was screaming.

With my school bag I banged on the arm-chewer's head, then the leg-chewer's. No effect. I tried kicking. They dug in harder. I found the biggest, sharpest stone I could, and with all my might, I smashed the dogs' hind toes, first one dog, then the other. They both let go, yelping. They backed off. One of the dogs had a white eye. Blind. I threw the rock and quite by chance, hit its other eye.

The dogs were gone faster than you could cry wolf. I didn't realize my own strength because lying near my sister was a bloodied dog's toe, its large claw distended. Maybe severing the toe was pure luck, especially since a dog's hind foot is smaller than its fore. One dog limped off with only seven toes holding up its back end. And one of them was blind. Maybe it was the same dog.

Beatta had evil bites on her legs and some on her arm, but she was okay. She had even less use for dogs now than she did before. The really weird thing, of course, was that after her wounds healed, she denied the attack ever happened. She remembered the "nose dog" but not the "leg dog," even though "leg dog" happened after "nose dog," when we were around ten. She didn't remember how she got the scars on her arm. It was around this time that Carl Danziger started following me home.

Memories don't die in chronological order, and I take it nothing is meant to live too long. I'm trying to get through grade twelve. Even though I swear these things are true, my mom says they never happened, that they are a product of my imagination.

Maybe so, but I know what happened the day before yesterday.

I went running after school over the first new snow of the year. Someone had been out earlier on their quad. Dog tracks trailed along beside the quad's. The only person I know who runs their dog while driving their quad is Carl Danziger.

Their tracks went only in one direction, so if they hadn't taken the trail around the lake, seventeen kilometers from where I normally enter the trail, I would have met them coming back. Meeting them always filled me with dread.

I had run nearly three kilometers, just about to my turnaround point, when I encountered a deer. A dead deer, newly dead, lying in a small clearing. The ravens had not yet found it. It lay a few feet off the trail. Blood was sprayed across the snow like red chiffon. I stopped and examined the site more closely. It looked like the quad might have hit the deer. A small hole trickled a frozen comma of blood at the center of the deer's skull, right between the eyes. Powder burns singed the fur around the hole. A large set of footprints showed that someone had walked around the carcass and stopped at its head. A second set of prints pocked dozens of dancing steps in and around the first. They belonged to a dog.

I turned around and ran back home.

Usually, I run till the snow gets too deep. Then I switch to cross-country skis. I don't like it as much as running free-footed along the trail, but I have to do something in winter. Skiing offers almost the same Zen-like experience as running, but skis are cumbersome and distracting, as much in their use as in their waxing and care. So I relish these last few free-foot runs before the deep snow comes.

Yesterday, another small layer of snow fell on top of the first. There were no fresh tracks, except those of a small fox meandering on and off the trail, and few squirrel runs. As I approached the site of the kill, a dozen ravens squalled, rising skyward, but the deer was no longer where it lay the day before. The snow, flecked black with droppings, was scuffed flat. An irregular path pressed into the shallow snow and grasses, snaking into the woods. I followed it till I came across what was left of the carcass. Then I realized it had been yanked there, inch by inch, because of the way the snow was ridged. It would have to have been something big, like maybe a wolf or a pair of coyotes. It was surrounded not only by raven prints but by canine prints of differing size and shape.

One of the prints had only three toes.

The whining of a two-stroke engine drilled its way through the woods. A quad was approaching.

x x x x x

My boss is Manny Delorme. The first week I worked for him, he gives me this quad. He took it as a payment for something, and it's a piece of junk, but if I get it going, it's mine. I can use it too. You don't need a driver's license for a quad—if you stay off the roads.

I get it going, and I'm as happy as a pig in you-know-what. So is Ike.

Ike's my dog. He's a great dog too, a German shepherd–something-cross but mostly shep. He could win shows if they had a German shepherd–something-cross category, except he's lost a toe on his left hind paw. Or maybe he was born like that. I don't know. He's also blind. He's got two white marbles for eyes. Maybe he can see shapes or light and dark, but not much else. I got him from the dump. I used to go there to shoot things, but not dogs. People leave pets there. They can scrounge food for a while if somebody doesn't pick them up and if the coyotes or ravens don't get them first. I saw a bag of kittens there once. I shot them. They were sick. I took Ike home, but Mom wouldn't let me keep him. That's how come I moved out. I was no good at school anyway.

The dog needed a name, and I always liked the name Ike because I saw this picture of a button in a book (or TV?) that said I Like Ike. I don't know who Ike was, maybe a politician or something, but I named my dog that right away without even thinking about it. Anyway, Ike loves going for runs with me on the quad. If I time it right, I get to see Maryanne Ravenhurst running too. Maryanne Ravenhurst and those long legs and long hair.

At work, I mostly do brakes and mufflers. Manny does the rest. I was working on a GM half-ton, only a couple of years old. I just replaced the brake pads, and Manny says, "Take it for a little spin to make sure they're set right." I'm thinking, *What if they're not set right, and I wind up in the lake?* And then I'm guessing that Manny can do without me, but not the business he would lose if one of his customers dies if his brakes don't work. So maybe I'm a bit ticked and I peel a bit of rubber around the corner, but I'm barely straightened out again when Constable Denis is flashing his red and blue cherries like the night's on fire.

"Hello," I says.

"Whatcha doing, Carl?" he says.

"Testing the brakes," I says.

"You stepped on the wrong pedal then. Where's your registration and driver's license?" he asks.

He knows my license is suspended, and he knows the truck isn't mine. He knows Manny's going to be really ticked if I don't get back fast. "This is stupid," I say to him.

"Better come with me," he says.

The last thing I need is another run-in with Denis. It wasn't even a month ago that he was giving me orders to destroy Ike, or he would be happy to do it himself. So I said, yes, no problem.

But I can't kill Ike. I love him. He needs me. I am his eyes.

I know where there's another dog around who looks just like Ike. So I find him, and I shoot him, and I gouge out his eyes and break off his jaw because it's a different color. Then I bring him in the RCMP office and park that dog right on Denis's desk, hoping the blood will run all over his nice neat stacks of paper.

Of course I have to be more careful about when I let Ike out and where I go with him. I stick to the woods, the lake trail.

So Denis takes me down to the cop shop and charges me with auto theft.

Manny is great about it, though. He doesn't fire me, and he tells Denis to take it easy, it's partly his fault, Manny's, for telling me to take the truck for a test drive. He tells Denis, by the way, to bring his car in, his own car, and he'll give him a real good deal on the winter tune-up special.

So Constable Denis, the tool that he is, brings his heap into the shop. Manny says to me, "It's all yours, kid. Don't screw it up." Only he doesn't say "screw."

This is not a big deal. Anyone can change the oil, rotate the tires and make sure the antifreeze is good to forty below—that's the special. So I do it, no problem. Okay, one problem: I forget to put the oil cap back on the cam cover accidentally on purpose.

After work, I take Ike for his run. Our usual track is once around the lake, about seventeen kilometers. I look forward to the run as much as Ike. Although he's in it for the exercise, I'm in it for the chance of spotting Maryanne Ravenhurst. Her dad owns Ravenhurst Supplies. I did a B and E there once. Maryanne's supplied, I can tell you that. Perfect. Sometimes I meet her coming, sometimes going, sometimes not at all. She never waves. She never looks at me. Which is just fine by me because I get to stare at her the whole time we're passing and she never knows. It's like I'm invisible to her. How do you get somebody to see you when they won't look? Maybe she's just blind, like Ike. Maybe she knows her way around these trails like he does. Sometimes he's gone for two whole days. Then he returns with a smile on his face and beer on his breath. He's been out partying somewhere. Okay, not beer—blood. He's been out hunting, but hey, that's partying for dogs. He dances around a kill.

Like yesterday I had an accident. I didn't think it was possible, but I was moving at a pretty good clip when I came into a small clearing and a deer got startled and jumped right into the quad. She was a small doe and badly injured. Somehow part of her broke open and sprayed blood all over. I knew I'd have to kill her, put her out of her misery. I put one bullet right between her eyes.

Ike danced the whole time. Danced in the blood.

I got back on the quad and kept going. Ike came with me for a little while, and then he disappeared. He didn't show up till this morning. My guess is that he went back to the kill. I'm curious to see it now.

There's a bit more snow this evening, and I can clearly see that Maryanne has been on the trail ahead of us. My heart beats a little faster. Part of me wants to see her without any clothes on, but mostly I just want her to see me.

So it was quite a surprise when I came into the clearing and there she was, standing near the woods. She looked up and waved for me to stop.

"Carl, come here!" she shouted.

I just about fell off the quad I turned so hard.

"Look at this," she said.

She was standing over the kill. It was hard to believe that in one day so little would be left of the doe. I became aware of a low growling. It was Ike. He was beginning to bare his teeth.

"Shut up, Ike!" I said. He backed off a bit, but he kept his forelegs locked stiff, ready.

"Did you kill this deer?" She asked. I suddenly was very visible to her. Naked. She looked me right in the eye.

"No," I lied, looking right back at her. I'm good at lying.

"I think you did. It looks like you ran over it and then shot it."

"I got better things to do than running over deer."

"You and that dog of yours. You just go around killing things."

"What's it to you?"

"You have no respect for things."

"I respect you. I think you're perfect."

"Go! Leave now," she said.

For some reason, her telling me this made me get off the quad. I didn't feel like leaving just yet. It was nice to have this conversation with Maryanne Ravenhurst. "You got real nice legs. From all that running, I guess, eh?"

"I'm going to scream."

"How about your feet? You got all your toes?"

"Yes," she said. She was real scared all of a sudden. She was taking little backward steps. But there wasn't far she could go before backing into the trees.

"Yes, what?"

"Yes, Carl."

"Call me Ike."

"Yes, Ike."

"Take off your shoes."

She stood there.

"I said take off your shoes."

"What are you going to do?" she asked. She was whimpering now. It was kind of pathetic, her hopping on one leg, taking a shoe off. First one, then the other.

"Now sit."

"Sit?"

"In the snow."

She sat. Ike was showing his teeth. Growling. "Shut up, Ike," I said.

"He can't see me," she said.

"No, he's blind. But he can hear good and smell better."

"I'm invisible to dogs," she said.

"But not to me," I said. "Now your socks."

"My socks?"

"I want to see your feet."

"They'll get cold."

"They'll get cold, what?"

"My feet will get cold, Ike."

"Ike," I said.

And that's when he went for her.

x x x x x

I thought the judge was pretty kind, considering the unusual viciousness of the crime and the fact that she might have bled to death. Manny did his best for Carl, trying to cover for him. Why he would even bother is anybody's guess. This time I shot the dog, the right dog, with those white orbs staring back at me.

The girl's going to be all right, but no more jogging for her. She was lucky she made it back at all, crawling all that way in the snow, her shoes gone, her toes chewed off. You wonder what the hell happened.

X X X X X

R.P. MacIntyre is primarily known as a fiction writer and editor. He travels extensively, giving his performance-like readings and workshops across Canada. He is currently on the editorial board of Thistledown Press and is acquisitions editor for YA fiction. He was born in Saskatoon, Saskatchewan in 1947 and makes his home in Candle Lake. He holds an Honors BA, English and Sociology, University of Saskatchewan, 1970.

Published works include the young adult novel, Yuletide Blues *(1991), and five collections of short fiction:* The Blue Camaro *(1994),* Takes *(1996—editor),* The Crying Jesus *(1997),* Up All Night *(2001—editor) and* Revved *(2002), all published by Thistledown Press. "The Rink" won the Vicky Metcalf Short Story Award;* Takes *won the 1996 Saskatchewan Book Award for Best Educational Book and 1997 Canadian Librarian Association Young Adult Book of the Year;* The Crying Jesus *won Saskatoon Book of the Year in 1998.*

THE YEARBOOK

Kathy Stinson

"What do you mean, Tara?" Our bus lurched through the knot of Saturday traffic approaching the mall. "Do you think Ryan is seeing someone else?"

Tara shrugged. "He seems so distant; I keep wondering if he's planning to dump me."

Angela yanked the cord to signal the driver we wanted off. "That would suck." The bus wheezed to a stop.

"Maybe he's just been preoccupied with final exams," Mercury suggested.

"I'd rather he was thinking about the grad dance," Tara complained. "He hasn't even mentioned it yet."

Together, the four of us scrambled down the steps of the bus to the sidewalk. Focused on Tara's boyfriend problem, we didn't notice the old woman shuffling by until Mercury practically knocked her over.

"Sorry." Mercury made sure the woman with her walker was steady, and apologized again.

But Angela, more impatient, said, "Come on, old girl, let's get a move on here."

"Never you mind, Missy." Whiskers on the old lady's chin bobbed in punctuation. *"You'll be old yourself one day. You'll see! You'll see!!"*

We all strutted away, across the parking lot, fake IDs in our purses, to the restricted movie showing at the mall cinema. Angela muttered, "Imagine that old bag going to see *Doing It?*"

"Or actually *doing it?*" I added, and we all had a good laugh.

In the lobby of the theater, electronic wails and crashes from the video arcades bounced off the walls in pulsing, pounding waves. Around the refreshment booths, flashing lights frenetically blinked.

"Hey look, there's Damien," Tara said.

We followed the strange boy from our English class into the darkness of theater six and sat two rows in front of him. I twisted round in my seat. "So, Damien, are you here to find out what 'It' is?"

Damien stared at me like the geek he is. "I know more than you think, Yardley."

"I'm sure you do, Damien. I'm sure you do."

Music blared, announcing coming attractions. I turned to the giant screen and gave no more thought to the loser behind us.

✗ ✗ ✗ ✗ ✗

Stepping out into the sunshine, my friends and I agreed that the feature had way less sex in it than we'd expected. Back at Angela's, we ordered pizza. She was clicking the remote through channels on her TV when Tara said, "Wait. Go back."

Angela flicked back to where a talk show host with mega-big hair was introducing her next guest, "—a psychic housewife from Newmarket, Ontario. Please welcome Mrs. Susan Meeks."

"I thought that's who it was."

"Who is it?" Mercury asked.

"Damien's mother."

We watched as she explained what people's auras communicated to her about their psyches, and how she used them to determine healing remedies like crystals and flowers for whatever ailed them. "Everything," she claimed, "from broken hearts to bowel obstructions."

"Oh, gross me out!"

"Feeling a little constipated? Here, dearie, how about a little tincture of violet?" Tara laughed.

"Man, no wonder Damien's such a weirdo," I said.

"You're not kidding."

"With a mother like that."

Of course, back at school on Monday, we had to give Damien the gears. "Do you see auras too?" Angela said. "What color is mine?"

"No, do me." Tara pushed herself forward. "I hope mine's green." She struck a pose as if standing still would actually help Damien see something.

"If you're feeling the need for green," he said, as if he—and we—took the whole thing seriously, "it means you're seeking peace and harmony."

"Hey, like with Ryan," Mercury suggested.

"Damien," I said, "maybe Tara would find peace and harmony if you managed for once not to be such a nerd." Everyone laughed. "Hey, does your mother have a flower remedy for geekiness?"

Damien just looked at me with the same stupid expression he'd had on his face when he said to me at the movie, "I know more than you think."

X X X X X

A couple of weeks later, our school yearbooks were ready to be picked up in the cafeteria. As soon as Angela, Mercury, Tara, and I got them, we flipped through to see how many times each of us appeared. None of us went for much in the way of extracurricular activities—not the kind they put in yearbooks anyway—

so it wasn't often. But in the pages of grad photos, we were all there. I glanced over a few of my classmates' captions, to see how they'd predicted what they'd be up to in the years after we all left this place.

'Signeury Watson will major in computer studies at Waterloo. Jasmine Wing will continue training toward Olympic gold in figure skating. Jamie Burns plans to bring solar power to third world villages currently without electricity.'

"Hey, Mercury," Tara said, "didn't you hand in a blurb saying you were going into teaching?"

"Yeah."

"That's not what's here."

Each of us quickly flipped to Mercury's grad shot, taken before she got her hair buzzed. Beside her picture it said: 'Mercury Rothchild will die peacefully in an assisted death facility with two grandchildren and a great-grandchild at her side.'

"Mercury Rothchild will die!" I said. "What kind of yearbook caption is that?"

"Maybe someone thought 'going into teaching' was a bit dry," Angela said. "Sounds like she'll live to be ancient, anyway."

"You too, Ange," Tara said.

"What?"

"'Angela Winters will die alone in an old-age home'—oh, maybe you don't want to hear this," Tara said. But she continued reading, "'—of a gangrenous bedsore the size of a grapefruit that will eat right into the base of her spine!'"

Angela laughed. "Yeah, right!"

"That's awesome!" I said.

Angela skimmed the pages of her yearbook. "Someone's messed with your entry too, Tara, and it looks like you won't live as long as me and Mercury."

"What do you mean?"

"'Tara Teasdale,'" Angela read, "'will die in a car crash the night of her grad dance, holding onto something precious.'"

"Oh, great!"

"That's only a week away," said Mercury. "Better live it up!"

"Maybe Ryan's going to give you a ring," Angela suggested.

"What about mine?" I said. It should say something about traveling in Europe while sorting out options for university. That's what I handed in, anyway."

"Let's see," Angela said, flipping pages again. "Beside your lovely smiling face, we have here . . . whoa, get this! 'Yardley Burrows will die of smallpox!'"

"Good one!" I laughed, and everyone joined me.

"I'd rather go early than end up like you guys," Tara said. "But what's all this death crap doing in the yearbook?"

"Yeah, and how come Mercury's the only one whose death doesn't sound absolutely gruesome?"

"Did you write this stuff and give it to the yearbook editor, Mercury?"

"Oh, sure, like I'd do that!"

"So who did, then?" I read out a few more captions. "'Inge Bordstrum will die of food poisoning.' Put her on our side. 'David Bowring will study sports medicine at Western.' 'Ming-Lee Crysler wants to marry a millionaire and raise a family of four in a mansion in the mountains.' Oh, jeez, listen to this: 'Ivan Dvorchuk will hang himself with his belt in a penitentiary while serving a sentence for murdering his own child.'"

"Ivan?" Tara said. "He seems like such a nice guy."

Angela smirked. "Isn't that what they always say?"

Nothing in the captions gave us a clue about who was behind them, so I flipped to the credits page. One name jumped out from all the others.

"Got it," I announced. "'Editor, Damien Meeks.'"

"Figures," Tara said. "So, has he got the hots for you, Mercury? Is that why he's letting you off easy?"

"He's just predicting our deaths," she said, "not making them happen."

Angela shoved her yearbook into her knapsack. "But how would he know about something like that?"

"He doesn't know, you idiot," Tara said. "He's just trying to bug people who've razzed him about stuff. Mercury probably just hasn't been as mean as the rest of us."

As we were leaving the cafeteria, Damien was coming in.

"Nice work," Angela said to him. "A bedsore the size of a grapefruit?"

"An assisted death facility?" said Mercury.

"And just when is it," I asked, "that I'm supposed to get smallpox?"

"In the image I get of your future," Damien said, "your face and body are so thick with pimples and blisters, it's impossible to tell your age."

"Oooo!" said Tara. "I wonder if you'll have them on your you-know-what."

"Gross me out!"

Everyone laughed. "Well, too bad you didn't do your research before you got your supposed image," I said. "You'd have found out nobody gets smallpox any more."

"Yeah," Mercury said. "Didn't Ms. Lynch tell us in grade six that it got wiped out years before we were even born?"

"What she didn't tell us"—Damien puffed up his chest as if he knew more than anyone about everything—"is that scientists kept some of the virus alive for research purposes."

"What are you going to die of, Damien?" Tara asked. "An excess of nerd genes in your bloodstream?"

"I've chosen not to know my future," he said.

"So, it was you!"

He shrugged. "Who else?"

It was all so stupid, what he'd done, but the expression on his face as he stood there in the hallway—so smug and even more full of himself than usual—ticked us all right off. As we neared the exit door, Tara stopped. "We should stick a few good Damien Will Die notices up on his locker. Pompous little—"

"Damien Meeks," I offered, "will burn to death—"

"After his marshmallow falls off its stick," Mercury continued, "and he tries to save it from the flames."

"Or how about," Tara suggested, "maggots will eat Damien's face off when he falls asleep after a romantic picnic with his pet iguana."

Angela hooted. "That's great! Except—what self-respecting maggot would go rummaging around *that* face?"

Behind us I heard a snicker. We turned. We thought Damien had gone into the cafeteria, but he'd followed us down the hall. I expected him to say something obnoxious, but the geek just shook his head, as if he thought he really did know something we didn't, and we were a pathetic bunch of kindergarteners who still believed in the Easter bunny.

Outside, Angela said, "I wish there was some way to prove how stupid that jerk's phony little predictions are."

"There is," Tara said.

"How?"

"Well, according to the yearbook captions, I'll supposedly be first to go knocking on death's door, right? The night of the grad dance?"

We all waited to hear her idea.

"So, I just won't go."

"You have to," Angela said. "No one misses the grad dance."

"It'll just make Damien think you're scared of his prediction, if you don't go," Mercury added.

Tara shrugged. "Ryan has to go to Ottawa to help his aunt move that weekend, so I was thinking of not going anyway."

"You don't believe this yearbook crap," I said. "Do you?"

"Of course not." Tara pressed the button for the light above the crosswalk. "But if I stay home from the dance, I for sure won't die in a car crash that night. That'll knock at least some of the wind out of Damien's maggot-faced sails."

The grad dance was a mishmash of music and heat, groping in dark corners, and as much drinking and smoking up outside as people could pull off with three teacher-chaperones milling around. It wasn't as good a party as ones we've had off school property, but I still hated that Tara was missing it. Especially since it turned out Ryan didn't have to go to Ottawa after all.

When things started winding down, Mercury suggested we walk home instead of taking a cab, or getting a lift with someone who might have been drinking, and no one argued. Maybe, even though we were sure Damien's predictions (or his mother's or whatever!) were just some loser's fantasy, there was also some sense of "what if it's not all total BS and the wrong girl stayed home?"

Angela was a bit high and didn't want to face her parents, so she came home with me. We decided to call Tara to assure her she really hadn't missed much. We agreed we wouldn't mention that Ryan had been there and spent most of the night dancing with Signeury.

When the answering machine kicked in, I hung up. "She must have gone to bed early."

"We can try her again in the morning." Angela flopped on the couch in my basement and bared her stomach to the breeze floating in the doors to the patio. "He doesn't know anything," she said. "Does he?"

"He who?"

"Damien. I never pictured myself old before, never mind all alone in some old-age home. I keep thinking about that bedsore."

"Oh, Angela, Damien is just a dumb geek with a psycho mother."

"But remember that old lady who yelled at me?"

"What old lady?"

"At the bus stop the day of the movie. Remember? She said, 'You'll be old too some day, you'll see.' She said it twice, Yardley, and the second time, she practically shouted. It was like she knew what Damien knows."

It was the dope talking, making Angela paranoid. "Damien knows nothing."

"He volunteers at an old-age home after school, you know, not far from the theater. I bet it's where that old lady lives. Yardley, they probably—"

"Stop it, Angela. The smoke's messing you up. Let me go make you some coffee."

"Yardley, I don't want to die."

"You're not going to."

"Yeah, I will. We all will."

"Shut up!"

As I waited upstairs for the coffee to brew, I wished Mercury were here. She could do a better job of snapping Angela out of this kick she was on than I could. I stirred lots of milk and sugar into two mugs of coffee and went back downstairs.

Angela was asleep. I drank both cups and watched the moon inch its way across the night sky.

X X X X X

I woke to the sound of the phone ringing. I dragged the receiver across the arm of the sofa to my ear. Angela was still out cold in the armchair across the room.

"Yardley, it's me. Did you hear about Tara?"

"I just . . . woke up." It was Mercury. I tried to sit up, but my head felt too heavy on one side. It fell back to the arm of the sofa. If Tara had heard about Ryan and Signeury from someone, I didn't really care. I just wished I had a glass of water.

"She's dead, Yardley."

Certain I'd misheard, I forced myself to sit up.

"While we were at the dance," Mercury went on, "her dad had an accident with his table saw. He somehow got his hand right under the blade. Took off three fingers." She was talking too fast. Why was she telling me about Tara's father? Maybe she hadn't said what I thought she had. "There was no one else home. I guess with all there's been in the news lately about how frigging long it takes an ambulance to come, she must have figured she'd better take him to the hospital herself."

Suddenly, what Mercury was telling me pounded me in the gut. I wanted her to stop talking, as if that could undo what I now knew had happened. Across the room, Angela was waking up.

"In her panic to get him there—imagine the blood if he cut off three fingers?—she took a corner too fast. She . . . collided . . . with a bus . . . head-on."

I must have repeated "head-on" because Angela started shaking me. "What do you mean, head-on? What are you talking about?" But she was crying, like she'd already figured it all out.

Into my ear—I was still clutching the phone—Mercury said, "They found his fingers bundled inside a rag. Tara was clutching it in her lap when they pulled her out of the car."

x x x x x

I'd always figured the stuff about fate, that ancient people bought into in those stories we read in grade nine English, was just a load of crap. And Tara's death, I tried to convince myself, was nothing but a fluky coincidence. But I don't know.

According to most of the Web sites I visited (I just couldn't get into studying for exams), smallpox is the most serious bio-terrorist threat in existence. An "event," some day, is almost certain. Even sites dating back before 9/11 say a lot of countries are manufacturing vaccines, preparing for that day. But there's no way there'll ever be enough to go around.

Smallpox pustules (even the words that go with this illness are disgusting) are big and hard and the scabs that form, mostly on your face and hands and feet, are even uglier. One site showed pictures of all the stages. There's a bloody form of smallpox too. With it, the linings of your throat, intestines, rectum, *etcetera,* disintegrate. Big slimy tubes of your insides come sliding out of you and you're actually still conscious when it happens. Apparently scientists are cooking up some super-pox that combines different strains of the disease that has already killed more people in the history of civilization than any other. Statistically speaking, I'll be in good company.

I log off the computer and step onto the sunny patio with my yearbook. It feels weird to see among all the cheerful grad blurbs, 'Yardley Burrows will die of smallpox,' knowing it's true. I look up from my picture to see Angela unlatching the gate to my yard.

She pulls up a patio chair beside me. "I went over to Damien's and told him I'd give him anything if he'd just let me die suddenly and without having to know ahead of time how it will happen. I meant it too—anything."

I'm ticked that it hasn't occurred to Angela that some of us just might be worse off than she is. So, she'll get a humongous bedsore on her ancient backside. How would she like the equivalent on her face, not knowing when it would happen? With that kind of certainty and uncertainty, I don't even know how to live any more. "So, did he take you up on your offer?"

"He said he can only *see* the future. He can't change it." Angela looks so scared I almost start feeling sorry for her.

Almost. "You've got years to live before you'll die, and sure it won't be pretty, but has it occurred to you that I have no idea when I'm going to end up covered with stinking scabs and pustules; only that I will? It could happen next week!"

Angela looks at me as if my face is oozing pus as I speak.

"Remember how people freaked last summer, when that epidemic of whatever it was broke out? Imagine what it will be like for me when—not *if*, but *when*—they announce the first case of smallpox."

" I . . ."

"Angela, this morning I was thinking, what if I'd rather kill myself than wait for what's coming? But you know what? It's like what happened to Tara was Damien's way—or maybe even God's, I don't know—of showing us that what the yearbook said about how we're going to die. . . . We can't escape it. I can take all the pills or slash away at my wrists all I want, but—"

Angela nods. "But something will happen so it doesn't work."

"Right. Because it's my destiny that my skin will slide off my body in stinking, bloody sheets!"

Angela jumps up from the patio chair and runs from the yard.

✕ ✕ ✕ ✕ ✕

When I show up at school for exams, people are still pretty hyped about the revised yearbook captions and Tara's accident. Which doesn't totally surprise me. What does is that there are actually people going on about how cool it would be to know exactly how they'll die. As if—in spite of what happened to Tara—they think *they* aren't really going to die at all.

The way Damien looks when they say stuff like that . . . ? I don't want to see next year's yearbook.

If I'm still alive when it comes out.

✕ ✕ ✕ ✕ ✕

Many of Kathy Stinson's more than twenty titles for toddlers, teens, and in-betweens have been published both in Canada and abroad. Several have been nominated for various readers' choice awards. Before becoming a writer, Kathy worked as a mail sorter, a waitress, and a teacher. She has enjoyed meeting readers all across Canada, and in England where she took part in an international exchange of children's authors in 1987. Born in Toronto in 1952, she received a Bicentennial

Civic Award of Merit from the City of Scarborough in 1996. Kathy currently lives and writes full-time in a small hamlet near Guelph, Ontario.

GOTH PATE

Carolyn Beck

DAY ONE

We are hanging at my locker watching the parade of girls streaming
in and out of the blue door to the girls' washroom. The hall around
us is packed, a jostling veldt of migrating species. End of lunch hour.

"Location, location, location, you lucky jerk." Ken grins
broadly. His eyes moon into slits behind his horn-rimmed glasses.
"Dunc, I'm going to spend a lot of time visiting you and your
locker this year." This is all talk, of course. The closest we three
fringe dwellers ever get to a girl is in our dreams.

"You're so lucky, Dunc," Alex moans. He gives his blond curls
a dejected shake. "My locker's way down at the other end, next to
George Heartwell's."

"Heartwell's?" Ken and I groan in sympathy.

Alex nods.

"That *is* creepy." Ken grimaces. "How long's he been missing?"

"It's gotta be a month." I shrug uneasily. George was in my Bio
class last year.

"It's like an empty coffin staring at me every time I . . ."

Alex's words, the blue door, the shouts and chatter—everything falls away. Out of the mist, out of the dust and chaos of the milling herds, appears Sonya Gutteridge. Plain, shy, bookish Sonya. A background person. Like us. Except . . .

"Is that . . . ?" Ken whispers, reverence in his voice.

Sonya has changed. She's gone Goth. Head to foot. But not the dead kind. She's alive all right. Silky black hair. Pouty black lips. Miles of leg disappearing up inside a short, tight skirt. And a little lacy top that's just about ready to pop. Va–va–va–vamp.

Alex and I do not respond to Ken's question. I don't know about Alex, but I've forgotten how to breathe.

She pushes at the blue door with one hand, tucks a finger of hair behind an ear with the other. Her fingernails are long black talons with sparkles. She's a Goth with flair. As the door yields, she turns, catches us, three deer in her mascara-rimmed, Goth headlights. Electric blue zaps through us. A quick smile of her black pouty lips, then gone.

"What happened to her?" I'm breathing again.

"Something good." Ken runs his hand over his buzz cut.

We stand, three rocks in the turbulent currents of the noonday migrations. Waiting.

After an eternity, a never-ending string of other girls, Sonya swings out the door, tall, dark, delicious. Not a glance in our direction.

We watch her sashay away from us.

"Outta sight," Alex blinks.

"Absolutely," Ken agrees. "Waaaay outta sight. . . ."

"Yeah," I sigh. "Waaaay outta our league."

Then the bell rings. And that is that. Close the book. Slam the door. Back to real life.

x x x x x

DAY TWO

The three of us are parked in our customary corner at the back of the lunchroom. The volume in the room is on high. A school filled with kids eating lunch.

We're doing algebra with our plastic cheese on white sandwiches.

"Y equals one slice of bread," Alex hypothesizes. "And X equals one slice of cheese."

"Therefore," I continue, "two Y plus one X equals—"

"One lousy sandwich," Ken takes a bite despite his conclusion.

"How 'bout," Alex starts coughing like something's gone down the wrong pipe, "Y equals one heavenly body, and"—cough—"X equals one tight leather skirt. . . ."

Ken and I look where Alex is looking.

There she is again. She's feeding coins into the drink machine.

"I think I'm in love. . . ." Ken speaks for all of us.

The drink thunks down.

As Sonya bends to get it, her short skirt rises to a new horizon up her black stockings. It's not the only thing rising in this lunchroom.

Sonya straightens, looks about. A few boys in her immediate vicinity have lost track of what they are eating, mouths locked mid-chew. She is a stunner.

She sees us. It's like—Snap! Click!—and she's heading our way.

Can't be. Okay, we've spent our prior lives inhabiting the edges of the school social scene, she as a mouse, us as just plain no-names, but that's not enough of a connection to explain what's happening right this second.

She's winding through the maze of tables and chairs and kids, blue eyes like laser beams on our corner. My heart starts beating to the slow, liquid rhythm of her hips. She's coming. I want this to be true. And yet I don't. She's ignoring the No. 1 Law of Nature: "in" folks do not sit at our table. It's a DNA thing.

"This seat taken?"

All three of us sit like dummies, our mouths gaping at the impossibility of this question.

"I'll take that as a no." She slides her heavenly body into the vacant chair. A harsh musky scent mushrooms around us. Goth perfume, I guess. No matter how gross it is, I'll do anything to keep breathing it.

She dips her black-nailed fingers into her bag and extracts a wrapped sandwich.

"I'm Sonya Gutteridge," she says with a toss of her raven hair.

"Yeah, we know," I reply dumbly. I love the way some of the ends of her hair slip inside the lacy edge of her top.

"And you're Ken Legerton, Alex Armstrong, and Duncan Dickinson right?"

I shiver to the sound of my name on her lips.

She starts munching on some kind of shredded meat in a pita pocket. We watch the motion of her jaw, the angle of her fingers on her sandwich, her every twitch. She is breathtaking. She is beyond breathtaking. She is brain-taking, heart-stealing, soul-sucking.

"You sure have changed," Alex blurts out.

"Glad you noticed." Her eyes sparkle. Her smile glistens.

The lunchroom is buzzing and clattering around us. The silence at our table is deafening.

And stupid, I realize suddenly. This is our chance. One in a million. A genetic mutation.

"So," I say intelligently, "how was your summer?"

I bathe in the sunshine of Sonya's smile. *"Special."* She breathes the word like it's the biggest secret in the world. "My parents moved to Whitehorse with my brother."

"Whitehorse, huh?" (Me, Einstein.)

"But you're staying here?" (Alex, genius of deductive reasoning.)

"With my Granny and Grandpa," she answers sweetly. Candy apples.

"How come?"

"You know." She shifts in her seat, smoothes her skirt. "Last year of school. They thought a big move might affect my grades."

"Oh, yeah." (We are brilliant conversationalists.)

She takes a long drink of her diet cola. I watch her throat open and close to the drink, hear her swallow. Then a quick lick, red tongue along black lips.

"Hey." She sweeps her hair to one side, exposing the length of her neck. "Would you guys like to come over to my place after school?"

Pinch me.

"Sure," mumbles Alex.

"Sure," mumbles Ken.

I've only got the strength to nod.

Her eyes flash, those magnetic baby blues. "125 Toomsbury. Come by around four-thirty."

Where are we?

Oh, yeah. The lunchroom.

x x x x x

Sonya lives in a white clapboard bungalow with green trim, a neat garden, and a doghouse on the side.

"Come in." She greets us with a little nervous laugh.

We step into the smell of fresh paint (like, really fresh) and blackness. The inside of the house, all the walls and ceilings, has been painted black. I wonder for a second how her grandparents would allow such radical décor. But just for a second. She's beckoning us into the living room.

"Have a seat, boys." Black leather furniture, black carpet, blinds drawn. She switches on some floor lamps that give off more of an amber glow than real light. You'd never know it is a sunny day outside.

"Make yourselves comfortable. The house is all ours. Granny and Grandpa have gone to Alaska—a cruise," she smiles.

"Lucky them." Ken settles on the couch.

"I'll be right back," she says, and we watch those liquid hips glide from the room.

I choose a chair by the fireplace. Alex decides to share the couch with Ken. I know we are all wondering where Sonya's going to sit.

We sit like statues in this strange, dark room. It's dead quiet and kind of naked. Just the furniture, the rug and the lamps, a TV, a stereo. No pictures or knickknacks. And, of course, there's the smell of paint. It's so strong it's burning the back of my throat.

There's another smell too, I realize, underneath the paint. A tiny stink. Like a small pile of week-old garbage. Just a whiff. Here, then not.

Ken giggles nervously. "You and your white socks, Dunc." He rolls his eyes in mock disgust.

Alex titters.

"Better than yours!" I retort. Kenny's been the mismatched sock king for two years running, his statement against the artificiality of fashion. Tucked inside his loafers today are one red and black polka dotted foot and one green and blue striped one.

"I'll say," Alex agrees.

End of a stupid conversation. We all look at Alex's plain black socks.

Alex shifts his weight on the couch. "X equals an empty house," he whispers into the quiet of the room. "Y equals a beautiful girl. Z equals a lonely boy. What's the equation for heavenly bliss?"

"X plus Y plus Z," Ken whispers back.

"So what's X plus Y plus three Z?" I ask.

No one replies.

Sonya pops back into the room with a tray of crackers and spreads. "This is a little pâté from Whitehorse," she explains, "compliments of my mother. And this is Alaskan. Help yourselves."

She crosses to the stereo and puts on some heavy organ music, like *The Phantom of the Opera,* only darker. Gothic, I smile to myself.

"It's kind of cool that Granny and Grandpa aren't here." Sonya flops herself into the chair across from mine. I would be able to see right up her skirt if the light weren't so dim. "I don't know about your grandparents, but mine are pretty uptight."

"How 'bout this paint job," Ken gestures around the room. "Forget grandparents—this would freak my parents out."

"Oh, they haven't seen it. . . ." Sonya crosses her legs. "Yet," she adds in response to our baffled stares.

I am reaching for the Whitehorse pâté, Alex for the Alaskan when my cell phone breaks into William Tell. Who can that be?

"Duncan?" It's Mom, and she's sounding mighty shrill. *"Where are you?"*

"I—"

"Have you forgotten?"

Have I forgotten? Key words to launch into panic mode. "I . . . uh . . ." I'm in major doo-doo, and I don't know why. Yet.

Sonya flashes the most radiant smile. For me. Just for me. I am sure. That smile empties my brain. The bowl that is my skull has been vacuumed clean. Not a fleck of dust in it. I inhale a lungful of black paint tinged with trash.

"Duncan! Jan's birthday?" Mom's squawk stabs my eardrum. Which is a perfectly appropriate way of reintroducing the thought of my sister back into my memory banks.

"Oh—Jan! I'm on my way, Mom!"

I've got no choice. I'm in enough trouble without saying, "Forget Jan's silly birthday with all her immature little friends, Mom. I'm hanging with Sonya."

This is a crushing blow.

"Sorry, guys," I say, sorrier that I've ever been in my whole life. "Gotta go."

"Oh no, Duncan. Do you?" Sonya mews. My name floats off those pouty black lips. Sweet agony.

"I do," I pledge my allegiance to her.

"Too bad."

"Sure is."

Ken and Alex are beaming from ear to ear. More for them.

All the way home, I imagine what I'm missing.

✗ ✗ ✗ ✗ ✗

DAY 3

Alex is at school. Ken's not. Nor, it appears, is the Goth Goddess.

"So?" We're at my locker. Just in case. "Whadya do?" Cool as a cucumber still on the vine. Worms of jealousy tunneling away inside.

Alex shrugs. "Not much. We hung around and listened to that organ music. It got so deep and boomy we had to shout. She made us supper. Anita's Meatloaf, she called it. She may look good, but cook good she can't. Of course, Ken and I competed for seconds and thirds, just to be polite."

"Ah, yes," I nod. Come to think of it, that pâté did look a little odd. But I would've wolfed down the whole thing if I'd had the chance. To be polite.

"After that we just hung around and watched TV, then split around seven-thirty, eight. I took the bus. Ken decided to walk."

"That's it?"

"What do you think?"

I'm thinking, why did I lose all that sleep last night thinking about what I thought they were doing?

"So where's Ken?"

"Beats me."

Half an hour later, we're called down to the office.

For what, we're joking. Sinful thoughts?

It's the police. In their stiff blue uniforms, guns hanging at their hips, the two officers ask us about our friend Kenny Legerton, that sunny-faced guy with the buzz cut and the mismatched socks who never made it home last night.

✗ ✗ ✗ ✗ ✗

I'm grabbing my Chem text and my Math stuff. I've got a ton of homework to do. Alex, the lucky jerk, had two spares this afternoon. He took off two hours ago.

I'm still thinking about what he said at lunch. He was freaking out about Ken. About having his locker next to Heartwell's. And about how clueless the police seemed. Then he stopped ranting and looked at his feet. "Ken was"—he swallowed hard—"*is* such a good friend." He looked up. "You are too," he said. Then he hugged me right there in the middle of the crowded hallway. Someone clapped. Someone whistled. A whole bunch of people smiled. But they didn't get it. They were on the inside looking out.

I slam my locker shut. I'm going straight home. Fat chance I'll get any homework done.

"Hi." It's Sonya. So she is here. She's got a big belt on and a long-sleeved dress that clings to every one of her perfect curves. Black gloves. Thigh-high boots. Very Goth.

I can feel eyes on us. That No. 1 Law of Nature. But who cares? I'm drowning—in Sonya's ocean.

"Any word on Ken?" Her whole face is aching for some good news.

I shake my head. The thoughts I've been pushing away all day come at me in one big, painful stab: Ken bound in chains, Ken threatened by knives, and other stuff that's much worse.

Sonya's mouth is all pouty and sad. She can feel my pain. "Do you want to talk about it?" Her sweet baby blues are brimming with tears.

"How about a cup of coffee?" It just slips out. She seems like the coffee type. Black, no sugar. I don't drink the stuff, but I'll choke it down for her.

Sonya's eyes are lost for a second, swimming too deep. Then she surfaces and smiles, mouth wide. I can see all the way to the back of her throat. What I'd do to be swallowed by her. "Duncan." She takes my hand. I almost melt right there into a puddle in front of my locker. "I'd rather go to my place."

The cells of my fingers are touching her glove. Through my hand I am connected to that lovely mouth of hers, her gorgeous eyes, her endless legs and that cleavage smiling at me from the top of her dress. I bet she's wearing black undies too.

Or none.

"Please."

"Yuh." I manage to utter.

"Great!"

It's my turn.

x x x x x

Going into her house again is weirder than the first time. The fact that the black walls and the strong smells are familiar feels odd to me.

"Make yourself comfy." Sonya motions to the couch. Her tongue makes a little tail out of the word "comfy." Like it's something delicious.

I lower myself suavely to the black leather couch, but as I lean back to cross my legs, cool, manlike, my stomach makes a sudden lurch toward my throat. Here I am, Duncan Dickinson, alone with Sonya Gutteridge. What am I going to do with her? Seriously?

"Do you want something to drink?" she asks. "I only have—"

William Tell charges into action.

It better not be Mom.

What crime have I committed this time? Well, it doesn't matter. I have Sonya all to myself, and nothing, I repeat, nothing, is going to drag me away from here.

"Dunc?" It's a far, far away voice. Down a well.

"Yeah?"

"It's Alex."

Sonya, still waiting for my drink order, starts to fidget.

"What's up? You don't sound so great."

"Where are you?" His voice is gray, like he's been shot in the stomach or something, and he's slowly bleeding to death.

"Ah . . ." I'm Alex's friend and all, but some things are best left unsaid. *My turn.*

"Are you at Sonya's?" Whoa! ESP.

"Uh huh."

Silence. All of a sudden Sonya's scooched up beside me on the couch. Her perfume envelopes me. Barbed wire and silk.

"Get out." A hard scratchy whisper. "She's doing us one at a—" Rattly breathing.

"Hey," I ask my friend, "have you seen a—"

Sonya's nuzzling close. Her legs, still sheathed in those sexy boots, fold up against my thighs. Her gloves flutter up and down my arm. My world is expanding at warp speed.

"—seen a doctor, Alex?" *I'm* going to need a doctor if Sonya keeps going.

"The . . . the . . . don't—"

Sonya grabs my phone and snaps it shut. "I'm getting lonesome," she whispers. Her eyes flare like blue flames. As she slips the phone back into my shirt pocket, she gives my ear a little nip. Her hair feathers my face.

I am twisted up so tight I think I'm going to pop. Here I am alone with the sexiest girl in the world. And Alex has to phone. And then there's Ken. Those awful pictures start flashing through my head again.

"Don't you worry about Alex," Sonya mews. "Just pretend he's in Partsville, Saskatchewan."

"Saskatchewan?" I should be giving those luscious black lips a little kiss. Instead I think I'm going to throw up.

Sonya pulls back, unfolds her legs. I'm losing her. Stupid. Stupid.

"I'm going to get a drink. Want something?" She plants a peck on my cheek. More barbed wire and silk. Hope.

I gotta hold on. Get a handle on things. "Do you have anything fizzy? Ginger ale? Cream soda?" Something to make me burp.

"All I've got is my home-brewed root beer. It sparkles." Just like me, her smile says.

"Okay. I'll try that." I sit in misery, wanting to seize this opportunity the universe has presented, yet . . . what was Alex babbling about?

Sonya returns with some of her Whitehorse pâté and two glasses, a black one for her and a bright yellow one for me. In the dimness of the room, my glass glows. The drink in it is the color of cranberry juice. It's bubbling all right, like bugs on a pond.

"*. . . such a good friend. You are too.*" Alex's words.

"I gotta go," I tell Sonya. Goddess or not, Alex is my friend, my only one right now. "I'll finish my drink, then, I'm sorry, I have to take off. I . . ."

"It's okay," she shrugs and sits beside me, close but not touching. Everything feels black and sour now.

I gulp down my drink. It tastes like root beer all right, like dirty-tree root beer. Alex was right. A cook Sonya's not.

"Sorry about this." Sorry is not the word.

Sonya nods in sweet understanding.

I push off the couch away from Sonya and the chance of a lifetime. My first step is okay, but the next is a little wobbly. Whoa. All of a sudden my joints go real loose. My body's trying to tell me something. "Could I use your bathroom before I go?"

"Down the hall." She's smiling that big tonsil-flashing grin.

Whoa. Down the hall I go, trying to be cool. I'm so dizzy I have to touch the wall along the way. Maybe I'll call a cab.

In the bathroom I use the sink for support. I look in the mirror. It's me. Ordinary old Duncan Dickinson. I look okay. But I feel like a wreck. All the stuff about Ken must be catching up to me. Or maybe I'm coming down with the same thing Alex has. Man, it hits fast.

I exit the bathroom. My total brain power is aimed at my feet now. One foot down, then the next. I hardly notice the garbage smell has gotten a lot stronger, and then I really notice. Like open sewer strong. I'm breathing cess. And my feet are sludging through thick sand.

I come to a door that has a handwritten sign taped to it. Saskatchewan, it reads. Loopy straight-up-and-down letters. A girl's writing.

Huh.

I don't remember passing any doors on the way to the bathroom. Where is the living room? I look back, head swiveling as slowly as the Hubble telescope in a space storm.

A-ha. I see. The discovery swims through my brain like a half-dead whale in mud. I've turned the wrong way. The living room is thataway. Dunky made a booboo. Boo hoo.

Something else starts galloping through my brain. A chain of ants, a thin, pesky parade of tiny feet itching from one side of my head to the other. Bill Tell again. He's in my shirt pocket. Too far for my hand to reach.

My hand, it seems, has accomplished the monumental feat of placing itself on the doorknob to steady my swaying body.

The door opens. What a handy hand I have.

The room is a stinking black hole. The stench in it slices up my nostrils like a thousand freshly sharpened knives, makes me think of the bin in the alley behind Malcolm's Meats on a hot day. The blackness is total except for a small glow to my left.

"Dunc." My name comes out of the darkness.

I want to scratch my brain. Bill Tell won't shut up.

"Dunc." Over by the glow.

My eyes start to decode the twisted shapes on the floor.

Huh.

Alex is here. One of his fair-lashed eyes is illuminated in the glow of his cell phone. The look in that eye, the way he's staring, pours into me like searing cold liquid.

His nose. The thought rises, a painful bubble, to the surface of my skull.

He must've dialed with his nose. Because my friend Alex Armstrong has no arms. Just black, jagged holes where his shoulders once were.

Pop!

"Duncan," Sonya is beside me. Her voice sends a wave of prickles across my scalp.

"No no no, Duncan." Her fingernails pinch at the skin on the back of my arm. She rips Bill Tell from my shirt pocket, and the chain of ants gallops no more.

"No. No. No."

The last thing I see as she shuts that door is a half-leg. The mangled knee-stub sits in a pool of blood on the floor, the red and black polka dot foot rests against the wall like a worn out flag. The loafer is gone.

She's pulling me farther into the stench. My nose ignites. My throat melts. My lungs vaporize.

We come to the end of the hall. Another door. There's no sign on this one. I'm propped against Sonya, legs two twigs now. Nothing matters except what I am supposed to be figuring out. But the thing I use for figuring is burned to a crisp. Brain toast. Ha.

The door in front of my teetering body opens. I feel Sonya's arm behind me, a sling of support. I hear humming.

A light flashes on. The brightness makes me squint. This room is all white. It is full of large white humming boxes.

"In you go." She steps away from me.

The slightest breeze will tip me over now. Instead, her foot does the job, a kick to my spine. I fall flat on my face.

If I could think, I might think my nose is broken, the wetness flowing from it, the way my breath clogs. I might think I have been kicked into a room full of refrigerators.

I hear the long unzipping of her boots. Clunk. Slap. They hit the cold tile floor my face is smashed into. There's a snap of latex gloves. Then the drag and knock of something heavy and metallic.

Her footsteps come back to me, soft pads across the floor. Her harsh Gothy scent leans over me.

"Duncan Dickinson." Even now I thrill to the sound of my name on her tongue. Lovely Sonya. With all my strength I turn my neck so I can see her. Something warm is running out my nose.

"Where shall we start?"

The first pull is a stall. The next brings a puff of smoke and a brain-drilling racket.

Chainsaw.

My guts writhe.

"Nuh." My protest putts out of my mouth as a small blood-bubbling fart.

"No, you are right." Sonya smiles that wide, toothy smile I love so much. "I don't need this." She shuts the chainsaw down.

In the sudden quiet, she rises and slips out of my range of vision. I am left staring at the handwritten sign taped to the humming box closest by: Whitehorse, it reads. The same straight loopy letters.

Huh.

Sonya is back. That smile. That gorgeous smile.

"Duncan Dickinson." She brandishes a pair of shiny new scissors. "These will do nicely."

X X X X X

Carolyn Beck grew up in Rosemere, a small town out-side Montreal, Quebec. A prize in third grade for her story "Petulia, the Petunia" cemented her dream of becoming a writer. But it wasn't until after many years of writing "for herself," developing a career in account-ing, and raising a family that Carolyn published her first book, The Waiting Dog, *a raucous, rhyming romp through a dog's mind (Kids Can Press, 2003).*

Carolyn continues to divide her time between free-lance accounting work and all sorts of interesting and unusual writing projects.

THE DEAD OF WINTER

Barbara Haworth-Attard

When we moved into our new house in July, Mom stared worriedly out the window at the river sliding smoothly by the end of our back yard.

"I don't like that river being there," she said.

"Well, I'll just see about moving it then," Dad told her.

Matt nearly fell off his chair laughing at that, so I did too, but Mom's lips tightened. "It's deep in the middle. And I heard there are holes in the bottom. One of those boys will fall in and drown," she predicted.

"They'll be fine," Dad assured her. "They both swim like fishes."

Matt made hollow-cheeked fish faces, and I copied him. Mom glared at all of us.

"Okay," Dad said hastily. "A couple of rules. You boys are never to go to the river alone, stick together, and you're not to go near it at all if it's running high."

We had a great summer vacation. We met some kids our own age two doors down, Justin and Terry, and canoed and fished with them, though Mom wouldn't fry up the fish we caught. "You eat those, and you'll light up at night or grow a third arm with all the toxins in that river," she said.

Matt said he'd like to have a third arm so he could swing a baseball bat and scratch his ass all at the same time. I wished desperately I was Matt—the older one, the one who made rude noises with his armpits and swore freely.

The river glided gently through the green of summer into the misty gold and red of autumn, then turned black with cold before freezing in a shimmering sheet in the dead of winter.

"New rule," Dad said. "You're not to go onto the ice until I check it every morning."

Matt groaned and rolled his eyes, but for once I didn't copy him. Matt could twist my arm until it broke, but I'd never let him know how the murky depths beneath the ice filled me with dread every time I looked at it.

Early one Saturday morning, Matt dragged Dad from bed and down to the river. Dad tentatively placed a booted foot on the ice and threw his weight upon it. It held. He shuffled out farther, stamping his heel as he went. "It's okay," he announced.

Matt whooped his joy. "Get your skates," he shouted to me.

As I sat on a log by the river and threaded the laces of my skates, my neck prickled. Straightening up, I caught a glimpse of a gray coat in the trees across the river from us.

"Who's that guy?" I asked Justin and pulled the laces tighter.

Justin threw a quick glance over his shoulder. "Who?"

I looked again. No one was there.

Goose bumps rose on my arms. Cold out, I told myself, better get moving to warm up. But my feet weren't too interested in skating any more.

"Come on, Tim," Matt called.

"Don't get your shorts in a knot. My skate doesn't feel tight enough," I lied. I bent down, retied the lace, took a couple of deep breaths and forced my foot onto the ice. Gaining confidence, I pushed off the snowbank with the other. The ice held firm. I pushed back the dread, pumped hard and was soon caught up in cold air, brilliant yellow sun, blue sky, and ice singing beneath my skates as I raced after the puck. Afternoon shadows slanted long when Mom called us to come in.

Matt gathered up the hockey sticks while Justin and Terry towed their net toward their back yard. I was bending to pick up the boots that marked our goal when white flashed beneath the ice. A fish, I thought. On hands and knees, I placed my face close to the ice to see better. Shooting up from the depths of the black water came white again. Then two hands slammed against the ice, fists first, then palms pushing, banging, desperate to get out. I fell over in shock.

"Auughh!" I screamed. "Matt! Matt!" On all fours I scrambled away. "There's someone under the ice! He's drowning! Matt!"

The boys threw down their sticks and skated quickly to me. Matt dropped to his knees, cupped his hands around his eyes and peered into the river.

"I don't see anything." He got to his feet and bent double, skated in widening circles as he searched the ice. "You're imagining things," he said. "Unless . . ." He came over and punched my shoulder hard. "You've having me on, aren't you? A big joke!"

"No!" I insisted. "I saw hands. They were trying to break the ice."

"Yeah, right."

Mom called again.

"Bring the boots." Matt skated away.

I quickly grabbed each boot, eyes averted from the ice. I didn't want to see those white, water-soaked hands again. I didn't bother to take off my skates, just plowed my way through the snow in the back yard. Halfway to the house, I turned, and there was the man in the gray coat, standing where I'd been, staring at the ice. He was old, fifty at least, stooped shoulders, wild beard. He turned his face to stare at me, and I hurried up the stairs into the back porch.

"Oooh, I'm drowning! Help me!" Matt jeered at the supper table. He laughed, giving everyone a clear view of mashed potato and peas in his mouth. "Tell them about the hands beneath the ice, Tim."

"What?" Mom exclaimed.

"Nothing," I muttered. "I just thought I saw someone underneath the ice. Probably a dead fish." I'd get Matt later, except . . . I wouldn't. I never did.

"We would have heard if there had been a drowning," Dad assured Mom. He glared at Matt. "Close your mouth while chewing!"

"I don't think you should skate any more," Mom said. "I don't think the ice is safe."

"It's thick, Mom," Matt protested.

I bet he wished he'd never said anything now. Serve him right if we never skated again. That thought filled me with relief. If only.

"We've had two weeks of freezing temperatures," Dad said. "It's perfectly safe. I check the ice every day before they go on. Besides, it's better they be out there than sitting on their butts watching television or playing on the computer."

His ace card. Mom hated us indoors. "Okay. You can skate. But remember the rule, Matt! Dad checks the ice first."

That night I dreamed of water-bloated bodies, hard ice above my head, and cries for help. I could barely keep my eyes open at school.

Matt rushed me home at the end of the day. "We can get a game in if we hurry."

"I'm too tired to play," I said.

"Wuss," floated back to me as he took off across the yard to the river.

I reluctantly followed and laced on my skates. A bleached log, I assured myself as I joined the game, but I had a hard time believing.

The puck came at me hard, hit my skate blade and shot off to the side. I skated after it and found myself beneath the overhanging branches of a willow tree, a cave of tangled yellowed leaves darkened by the late afternoon shadows. Fishing for the puck with my stick, I saw them again. White hands, pounding at the ice—and this time a pale face between them pressed against the ice, eyes wild, mouth open in a frozen cry of horror.

"Matt!" I shrieked. "Matt! It's him again. He's here. Help!"

Justin, Terry, and Matt came flying over, bent to look where I pointed, then straightened in disgust.

"There's nothing there. This joke isn't funny any more," Matt said.

Terry shoved me into the tree trunk.

I trembled from head to foot. "I'm going home."

Stumbling up the bank of the river back of our house, I felt a hand grabbing my arm. A figure loomed up before me. I yelped in fear.

"What did you see?" A face thrust into mine. Bearded. "What did you see?" the gray-coated man repeated, giving me a shake.

"Hands! Beneath the ice. And a face," I blurted out.

I wrestled my arm away and raced for the house. Reaching the door, I turned back, but he was gone. I stumbled into the house.

"I'm sick," I told Mom.

One look at my face and she quickly unlaced my skates, pulled off my coat, led me to the couch, and wrapped me in a quilt. A moment later a hot cup of chocolate was placed between my hands, but I could barely drink it, my teeth chattered so much.

"I saw the hands again," I told Mom. "There's a drowned boy."

A short time later, two police officers stood over me, one old, one young.

"We've not heard of anyone missing," the older man said. "Been fifteen, nearly sixteen years since we had a drowning here. I hadn't been on the force too long when it happened. Harry McPherson. He was twelve."

"You could ask that man," I said.

"What man?" Mom asked.

"There's a man that walks along the river. He's got a beard. I think he's looking for someone. He wanted to know what I saw."

The older officer shot me an odd look, but said nothing more.

They moved into the kitchen, and I heard the younger one telling Mom they'd check with the police up the river, but it was probably a dead fish I saw. As they left, I heard the door close, but it must not have latched shut because I clearly heard the older officer say to the younger one, "You know, they never did find that McPherson boy."

"No more skating," Mom said at supper. Matt was so mad he drew a line down the middle of our bedroom with chalk and told me I was never to cross it.

Terror came with the night. White hands, wild eyes, then me beneath the ice, water in my chest, screaming . . . screaming. Mom kept me home from school the rest of the week. "I knew he'd get chilled being out so much."

"But Mom, you're always telling us it's healthy to be outdoors," Matt told her.

"Be quiet, Matt," she said.

Saturday morning, I woke abruptly, nightmares jarring me from sleep as they had all week long. Footprints smudged the chalk line between our beds. Matt's was empty. I lay listening to a steady drip-drip and thought Matt was in the bathroom, then realized it was water running in the eaves. Heart pounding, I threw off the covers and pulled on my jeans. I knew where Matt was!

Grabbing my coat on the way out the door, I ran pell-mell across the yard. The air felt soft against my face, scented with melting snow. I could hear the swish of a skate blade and saw Matt stickhandling the puck across the ice.

"Matt!" I waved a hand.

"Get your skates, Tim. We'll play a little one-on-one," Matt yelled.

"No!" I scrambled down the bank to the river edge and saw a thin band of water where a few days ago had been ice. "Matt, the ice is melting. Come in."

"It's fine," Matt shouted, skating backward away from me. "Get your skates."

"No." It was the first time ever I didn't do what Matt wanted. "Get off the ice," I pleaded.

"You're such a—" A loud crack split the air. One minute Matt was there, the next he'd disappeared.

"Matt!" I screamed. I didn't know what to do. If I ran back to the house, Matt would be drowned.

"Dad! Dad!" I yelled as loud as I could, then I fell on my stomach and wormed my way over the ice toward the black hole where Matt had fallen through.

Water soaked into my coat, weighing me down. I shrugged it off. My heart thudded in my ears as I listened for another loud crack that meant I'd gone through too. Suddenly beneath me, beneath the ice, I saw hands, a face, but this time it was Matt, eyes wide with fear. He'd been pulled by the current from the open water. I pounded on the ice, trying to break it. Then another pair of hands came from below Matt and grabbed him and pulled him down. The other boy. The drowned boy.

"No," I screamed. I pounded the ice with both fists and it cracked. "You can't have him! You're dead! He's alive!"

The gray-coated man crawled up beside me. He shattered the ice with the flat of his palm, and we had a jagged circle of open water. The two boys floated up toward us, the one clawing at Matt, trying to pull him down.

"No," the man said firmly. "Harry. Son. You let him go."

A shake from the drowned boy's head. He wanted Matt. He wanted someone.

I could see bubbles coming from Matt's mouth. His arms had stopped flailing and floated lifeless at his side. "No, you can't have him!" I shouted.

The boy pulled Matt down into black water, out of view.

"Harry! You let him go! I know where you are now, son. You won't be alone any more," the man yelled.

A moment later, Matt's head surfaced through the hole in the ice, and white hands pushed him up. Mr. McPherson grabbed Matt beneath the arms and hauled him onto firm ice. A face floated just beneath the surface of the water. The man reached into the hole and gently stroked the face. "You're a good boy, Harry," he whispered.

Sirens. An ambulance, police cars, and a fire rescue truck. Dad and Mom frantic on the riverbank. A crowd gathering, and firefighters coming across the ice. Pulling us in. Working on Matt. As Dad wrapped me in a blanket, I turned around and saw Mr. McPherson still on the ice, staring into the hole. "Dad," I said. "He's going to fall through."

"It's okay, Tim," Dad said. "Matt's safe now."

"No. Not Matt . . ." I started. Then Matt was being loaded into the ambulance and Mom climbed in after him and the siren drowned out my words.

"Quick thinking, crawling out on to that ice on your stomach." It was the older police officer again. "You saved your brother."

"It wasn't just me," I said. "The old man I told you about. In the gray coat. He helped. Mr. McPherson. He pulled Matt out of the water. He's still out there." I pointed out to the ice, but my arm slowly dropped. There was no one there.

"It couldn't have been McPherson," the officer said.

"It was," I insisted. "He was looking for his son, Harry. The drowned boy. It was Mr. McPherson."

There was a long silence, then, "McPherson went a bit strange after Harry died," the police officer said. "He used to go up and down the river looking for his boy. Every day the old man searched." The police officer paused and looked out over the river. "Right up until the day he died. Five years ago."

X X X X X

Barbara Haworth-Attard was born July 25, 1953, in Kitchener, Ontario. Her fondest memory of childhood is going to the local library every Saturday afternoon. After completion of high school, Barbara worked as a legal secretary until 1998, while writing freelance non-fiction articles for local newspapers. Her first short story was published in 1993 and her first novel, Dark of the Moon, *in 1995. Since that time she has published ten novels for middle grade and young adult readers. Her books have been short-listed for a variety of awards including the* MR. CHRISTIE AWARD, *Silver Birch, Red Cedar, Red Maple, Geoffrey Bilson Historical Fiction Award and the Governor General's Award for children's text. Barbara lives in London, Ontario, with her family.*

SEPTEMBER 12, 2063

Martine Leavitt

I don't mind dying, son.

    Worst thing about it is seeing your face all old with being sad, and your sister running out of the room to cry. Especially if it's today, I don't mind. It's still September 12, isn't it?

I know what they've got going in this IV. I know it's Juice. They guilt you into this, son?

In a little while, I'm going to take it out. Don't tense up on me, I'm not doing it yet. I need to tell you something first, and then we'll see if you'll just let me reach on up and die natural the way we used to do before they invented this awful stuff.

Son, something happened to me this day, September 12, a long time ago, when I was nineteen years old.

I know you and I have different notions about religion—no, I'm not going to start on you again. I'm just going to tell you something that happened to me, plain and simple. I wanted to tell you so many times. I told your mama, and she believed me. She asked me to tell you, you and Anna. There never seemed to be a good time. . . .

It's different now. You know I wouldn't lie to you ever, but especially just before I'm about to meet God.

I was nineteen and I was way down. . . .

Wait. I guess the story really begins one day when I was twelve. For some strange reason your grandma took me to Sunday school. I remember it was a long time to sit, but I liked the music and my mom's arm around me. While I was there, the other kids and I went off with this old woman (probably younger than I am now). She took us into a classroom and talked to us about faith.

I didn't understand everything she said, but I understood that having faith made you into a kind of superhero. I mean, if you had faith, you could do anything, right? You could move mountains. . . .

That very afternoon I went to the river near our house, alone, and I stood on the steep bank. I stood there a long time. The river was brown and fast with spring run-off. If you fell into a river like that, son, you'd die. Sometimes kids even did.

I stood there and I thought, I won't fall in. I told myself I would fly to the other side of the river if I had faith. If I had faith, God would just float me on over to the other bank. He'd just hold me in the palm of his hand and plunk me . . . Well, you get the idea. I held out my arms straight at my sides. I hung my big toes over the edge. I teetered. . . . Faith . . . faith . . .

And then I sat down. Collapsed, more like, thinking about how close I'd come to drowning. That would have been a cold, suffocating way to die, son. But maybe no worse than stomach cancer.

Anyway, I scooted away from the edge, stood up and walked home, sad as I'd ever been. Seemed for a long time that was my last happy time, that morning in Sunday school, thinking about being a superhero, but I never went to church again. Mama never tried to take me again, anyway, though she often said she should have, I was such a rotten kid.

I didn't mean to be bad. I just didn't get life, and the older I got, the less I got it.

Seemed like some people got it.

Some people just did goodness like breathing. They smiled at their teachers. They thought about their futures, got an education, saved their money, dreamed about having a house and maybe getting married, having a kid or two. Some of my friends, they just lived and did all this good-life stuff and had a good time.

Me, I was different. I sat around wondering what it was all about and having issues.

My parents didn't understand me, and I didn't understand them. My dad went to a job he hated every day of his life just to provide shelter. On weekends he spent all his time tinkering with the shelter, grooming it, painting it, renovating it, tweaking it. He devoted his life to shelter.

My mom, your grandmother, devoted her life to food. She planned her life around supper. She studied cookbooks like they held the secret of life. She shopped twice a week and reorganized her spice cupboard and lined her oven with tinfoil and freshened and cleaned her fridge. She spent several hours a day making me good-start breakfasts and creative lunches and healthful-but-appealing suppers. This did not count all the time she spent doing dishes or the essential food celebrations like Thanksgiving and Christmas. My father would decorate the shelter weeks in advance of Christmas, and my mother would do her baking and plan her menu. But what were we celebrating? The birth of Jesus? Did we believe in Jesus? Or was he someone like Santa Claus, someone we all just liked pretending to believe in?

Well, one day after I'd graduated from high school, my girlfriend broke up with me, I went to work and lost my job, and my older brother phoned to say my nephew had just died in a car accident. All within twenty-four hours. You've heard me talk about him—sweet little kid. My mom cried a couple hours, and then she gets up and starts baking for the funeral. My dad, he goes straight over to my brother's house to mow the lawn and fix the gate. He's so sad, he ends up painting the fence.

I just couldn't stand the futility and uselessness of life one more day.

I decided to go. Didn't know where. Didn't care. I just knew I had to get away. I took out some Bristol board from my mother's hoard and wrote on it: Promised Land.

Then I hiked to the highway, stuck out my thumb, and held out the sign.

It was partly a joke.

It was partly that I thought everyone would see that I had a good sense of humor and would pick me up. I'd get rides quicker. I felt like if I didn't do something outrageous, I'd have to kill myself or something. And as I was standing there, running away, knowing my mama was planning her grandchild's funeral and would soon find out her son was missing, and realizing what a low-life I was, I decided that was the answer: I would kill myself.

Yes, son, I'm comfortable enough. Comfortable as you can be when your body is kicking your spirit out of it and there's some kind of high-tech cocktail keeping you alive.

But listen, now, because this story, I swear, is true. Every word. Would a man about to die tell his only son a lie?

Sometimes I think all the ingredients had to be there: the sign, the low heart, walking backward down the highway. And then it was September 12, 2003.

Anyway, I'm hitchhiking with this sign saying Promised Land, and people are grinning and a couple of them wave and honk. And I'm thinking this sign is making things harder on me when this car pulls over. It's a big, old, white Cadillac, with brassy wings on the tail fins. It was one of those old cars that makes you feel like you're sitting in a living room when you get in, all roomy and comfortable.

The old guy who's driving it kind of nods at me as I get in, and at first I swear I've got picked up by Johnny Cash himself, he looks so much like him. He's all in black, and there was the hair, and the mouth that makes you think he's mad but the eyes that make you think he's sad. Strange coincidence, I think, because I heard on the radio, before we knew about my nephew, that he died today. Seems like weeks ago to me. Johnny Cash and my nephew, same day. Same cursed day.

"Thanks for the ride," says I.

The man, he just barely nods his head.

Silent type, I think, so we just truck along together for twenty minutes or so, right through Nanton and on our way to Claresholm. At the time, Johnny was already a bit of a classic. I never would have thought that sixty years later my kids would still know his name. . . . Well, anyway, we're going along and finally I ask, "So, where are you headed?"

Man answers, "Same place as you, son." His voice is all deep and gravelly, just like Johnny Cash's voice.

"Claresholm?" I say. I laugh a little, but he doesn't laugh. He doesn't even smile.

Mental case, I think, and we just travel along together for another half hour or so in silence until we get to Claresholm.

He just sails on through.

After Claresholm, I'm thinking, there's Fort McLeod and Lethbridge, and then a whole lot of not much of anything for a good long while. Taber. And then . . . was there anything at all after Taber?

I'm thinking also, what am I going to do if he turns onto some gravel road and pulls out a knife? That wasn't my preferred way to die, though I didn't know what was.

I'm thinking this, but I'm not feeling it. I'm feeling safe, really, no negative vibes at all. My head is thinking that I'd better say, This is as far as I'm going, pull over here. But my gut is telling me to have a nap.

So I do.

Best sleep I ever had.

I wake up drooling, and I can see that we're headed to the mountains. He'd gone west after Fort McLeod, and there's the Blood Reserve and Cardston and then, if I'm lucky, Waterton National Park. Good place to die. I'd just walk off into the forest and get myself lost or eaten by a bear.

"Are you going to Waterton?" I ask.

For a bit he doesn't answer me, like I've asked him this really important question. Then he says, "Boy, I'm headed right to where you want to go: the Promised Land."

It dawns on me: there is a real town called Promised Land that I didn't know about.

"No kidding," I say. "A real place called Promised Land. Must be pretty small."

Silence.

"So do you live there?"

"I'm going there," the man says patiently.

He has this real slow way of talking that calms me. I feel like I can say anything to this guy, and it will be okay, like I can ask him for the meaning of life and whatever he says will be true.

"Say, I'll bet you've been told a thousand times that you look like Johnny Cash."

He sort of half grins and glances at himself in the rearview mirror. Then he looks in the mirror again, a little harder this time.

"Well, son of a gun," he says all low, as if he's talking to himself. "How about that? I haven't looked like Johnny Cash in a long time." He chuckles low and deep.

I don't understand what he means. "It's uncanny really," I say. "Amazing. You know, I've heard you can make a lot of money if you look like a celebrity. You should check it out, because, man, you look more like Johnny Cash than Johnny Cash does. Did. You look like him when he was a lot younger."

He says, "Son, that's because I am Johnny Cash."

Okay, so I'm in a car with a true psycho.

You'd think I'd be afraid. But, you know, I'm just not. I'm feeling better in fact than I've felt for a while. So I just settle in and grin and go, "Well, you don't say."

Now, Johnny Cash even then was already a legend of sorts. I had a few of his CDs at home and went to a concert of his once, and I knew a couple of things about him. So I decide, hey, the loony tune seems to be able to drive okay. I'll just have a little fun with him. I say, "So tell me, where were you raised, Johnny? Nashville?"

"No, son. I was raised in Arkansas. Moved to Dyess when I was about three years old. Sang on the Arkansas radio station when I was still in high school."

That was pretty good. There were lots of people who would've sworn he was born in Nashville. I mean, if you're going to impersonate a celebrity, best to know about the person. I say, "But then you dropped out, got in trouble with the law, traveled around with your guitar. . . ."

"No, son. I graduated from college, got to work and joined the Air Force during the Korean War. That's when I bought my first guitar and taught myself to play."

I'm thinking the guy is crazy, but he isn't stupid.

"So that's when you married June Carter?"

"Divorced the first wife before I married June. Before June— that was a sad time. Sad time. Got in trouble with the law, wrecked my body with amphetamines."

"That's what you got in trouble with the law? Drugs?"

Everybody thought Johnny had gone to jail for a barroom brawl. There were rumors he'd killed a man in defense of a girl.

"Nope," he says. "Started a forest fire."

The way he says it jolts me. He says it not like it's a fact he's memorized and not like a crazy person who doesn't feel things like other people do. He says it like he's sad for all those dead trees, like he's kind of ashamed even though it happened a long time ago.

This creepy, horror-movie-music feeling touches me at the base of my neck and fingers its way over my scalp.

"Something you may not know," I say loudly and snidely, "is that Johnny Cash died today. Early this morning."

Maybe I think I can cure him with the facts. Maybe I'm just being mean, trying to pop his bubble, see what happens to impersonators when they meet up with their own deaths.

I wait, but he doesn't even blink.

"Son, I know that," he says. "I was there." He says this in a real profound voice. "Dying ain't so bad."

He says it as if he's thinking it out loud, like it wouldn't matter if I heard him say it, like he's still kind of surprised.

"Oh, I see," I say. "So, what are you, his ghost or something?" My voice has got all sharp and sarcastic.

He grins lopsided, peeks at himself in the rearview mirror again, and says, "I prefer to think of myself as an angel."

Now, for the first time, he looks at me. My brain is on overload. I'm thinking, dear God, this *is* Johnny Cash! I'm thinking, if he's not crazy, I am. I'm thinking, isn't this all pretty damn hilarious? I'm thinking I'm hungry. I'm thinking, if this really is Johnny Cash, then maybe I'm dead too.

Johnny says, "You're not dead, boy, and don't you worry about me. I got religion."

Can angels drive? I'm wondering. Are they allowed to speed? "So, did you just fake your death to get away from the paparazzi?" I ask. Am I buying into his state of mind if I engage in a religious conversation with a bona fide nutcase?

He says, "Son, you have some real unkind notions about people with mental illness, and you should repent."

"Yeah, well, I don't believe in God."

"I know, son," he says. He says it (there's no other way to describe it) tenderly. "That's what this whole thing is about, isn't it."

He isn't asking. He's telling me.

"How do you mean?"

"You have to believe first, son. That's what the Good Book says, and that's been my experience. Beautiful day, isn't it?"

All I can see for miles around is yellow prairie, a shabby, gray farmhouse, ordinary clouds. The faint gray rim of the Rockies is just visible ahead.

Johnny clicks his tongue, ducks his head, and drawls, "Always makes me happy to go to the mountains."

Perfectly harmless, I think. I hope. "So, why did you pick me up, Johnny Angel?"

"Well, son, God told me to."

I laugh. "Guess you and him are on speaking terms now that you're an angel."

"Guess so." He grins. He seems almost too happy to be concerned with me. I'm like this project, something he has to do even though there's stuff he'd really rather be doing.

"And why did he tell you to pick me up? Was it the sign?"

"That was part of it. And also because of the mad part. God doesn't want you to be mad at him anymore."

I burst out laughing again. It feels good. I haven't laughed like this in a long time, but this whole thing is getting so stupidly ridiculous that I can't help myself. I get mean. "Look, old man, I told you, I don't believe in God."

"Oh, you do," Johnny says, all peaceful and calm. "You believe in him enough to be mad at him. You're mad because he doesn't make you believe in him. You're mad because he doesn't show himself. You're mad because he lets little kids die. You're kind of mad about this whole death thing, really."

Okay. Okay, son. Just let me get my breath.

Hold my hand, son.

I love you, son. That's the most important thing—even more important than this story. You've become a good man. I love you. Just so long as you know that.

Where was I?

No. I have to tell it.

Listen. You're going to think this is weird, son, but while Johnny Cash is saying all that, I know it is true. I'm realizing I do believe in God, but I don't want to just believe. I want to know for a fact. I want God to come sit on my bed at night and tell me why I should be a good boy. I want him to tell me that nothing bad is going to happen to me or anybody I love. I hated having to just believe.

"Okay, so what's with all this invisible stuff?" I say to Johnny. "Why doesn't he just show himself once a year in Times Square and end the debate? What's so great about having to believe?"

"Faith," J.C. says. "Faith is power. It's what spins galaxies and determines where quarks go and what makes the sun shine. It's how he made the universe. It's how he gets to be God. He wants you to have it. He starts you out small. He doesn't say to make the blind to see. He doesn't say to part the sea. He just says: believe."

The mountains are getting closer, and they're looming up so big that I can't take my eyes away. I tell the mountains, "I had faith once. For about five minutes."

"Yes," J.C. says. "The river."

I almost get whiplash when I swing my head around to him. How did he know about the river?

"Son, that's why you get me," J.C. says. "You get an angel because of that five minutes you teetered on the edge of that steep bank, teetered on the edge of faith. God's had his eye on you ever since. And son, he's gonna teach you something today. After that, the debt's paid—you do what you want. That's another reason why God's invisible too, to give everyone a fair chance at doin' what they want. You know, without feeling too obligated to whoever is watching."

Just then he turns down a side road, a gravel road. A brown sign says Horseshoe Canyon.

Suddenly I get my brain back.

This is it, I think. The old guy's going to pull a knife and kill me. Just thinking about it makes me mad. I mean, yeah, I want to be dead, but I don't want some old freak doing it for me. The only thing that keeps me from jumping out of the car is that he knows about the river. How the hell can he know about the river? Of course, it could have been any river. He could have said "river" to anyone and it might have meant something.

The farther we drive down the road, the madder I get, until it occurs to me that maybe I don't want to die after all—not by Freaky Johnny, and not by me, either. I'm thinking how disgusting and selfish it would be to hurt my mom and dad like that when they'd just lost a grandchild, or even if they hadn't just lost a grandchild.

While I'm thinking all this, the old man stops the car. I'm ready now, ready to fight for my precious, wonderful, amazing-though-so-far-crappy life. I pull on the handle, and I'm almost shocked when it opens. I leap out of the car, and air rushes into my lungs like I'm taking my first deliberate breath ever, and the old guy gets out too.

He's not looking so old anymore. He's been, like, getting younger or something as we drove.

He looks so much like Johnny Cash now I want to forgive him for being crazy. I mean, if I looked that much like Mick Jagger, I'd feel I had a right to *be* him.

Johnny is gazing around, so I do too, without letting him out of my peripheral vision. "So," I say, real cautious (no need to rile him if he isn't already riled). "So, is this the Promised Land?"

"No. This is Horseshoe Canyon."

He says it patiently, like I'm the crazy one. I feel myself blushing a little, but I also feel kind of relieved. He just doesn't sound like someone who's about to kill a guy in the next few minutes.

Then I see the canyon, and the river, and the falls.

All I can tell you is, it is real pretty. I mean to say, it's just bending my mind to see all that white water rushing and plunging like that. I'm thinking, you don't really know water until you see that much of it jumping out of its skin. And the mountains are as blue as the sky and the air smells sweet and clean.

Johnny says to me, "Son, here's your chance."

Here we go, I think, and my whole body tenses up. He's going to do his psycho number on me now.

But something inside me keeps me from running away and tells me that's my inner idiot talking.

"What do you mean?"

"I mean faith, son." He turns and faces me, and his thumbs are hooked over his belt, and the sun is so bright behind his head that I can hardly see his face clearly anymore. "Not too many people get to see an angel, son, and the only reason you get to is because of that day by the river when you were twelve years old.

"So now, here's your chance to do it again. Jump."

Oh.

He isn't a stabber.

He's a pusher.

"You are certifiable, you know," I say. "You should get on some serious medication. I'm going back to the main highway."

Johnny Cash doesn't answer. He just stuffs his hands in his pockets and looks around like he's already forgotten all about me and is enjoying the scenery. I'm just about to start walking away when he starts singing.

Singing.

Oh, Lord, you never heard such singing.

And in the way that only the real Johnny Cash could sing.

No.

Better.

Hear the trumpets, hear the pipers
One hundred million angels singing
Multitudes are marching to the big kettle drum
Voices callin', voices cryin'
Some are born and some are dyin'
It's Alpha and Omega's kingdom come
And the whirlwind is in the thorn tree. . . .

While he's singing, I'll be damned if I don't see this light shining around him, shimmering at the back of his head and fluttering behind him like wings. Maybe there is no light there, I tell myself. Maybe it's the setting sun playing tricks. Maybe I am so tired and down, I'm seeing things.

No.

This is Johnny Cash. And he's singing to me.

No.

I've gone completely nutso.

"Son," Johnny says real gentle, "you've got an unnatural fixation on mental health."

I hate for him to stop singing. The last note echoes over the roar of the waterfall. I go to him and throw my arms around him.

"It's just like in the movies, I swear, son."

My arms go right through him, like he's a big old hologram or something.

I step back.

Up until now he's been looking at me . . . like I was a fan, not seeing me too hard. Now, though, he's looking hard at me.

"That's real nice, son," he says kindly. "Now, I can't hug you in the usual way. But . . ."

Then I feel this warmth around me like someone just dropped a heated blanket on my shoulders. I feel the tears come pouring out of my eyes and nose.

"My nephew . . ." I begin.

He goes, "I know, son. I know. No words for that kind of sadness."

I know he feels the sadness with me.

"My girl broke up with me," I sob, and I'm ashamed that he'll know that that sadness hurts almost more than the first. He hugs me again.

I want to run, but there's no breath in me.

I want to drop at his feet.

I want to check myself into the nearest hospital. The whole scene, waterfall and all, rolls like I'm on a boat. I put my hands out to steady myself.

"Okay," I pant. "Okay. So let's say for a minute that I'm not insane and you really are an angel. What do you want from me?"

Johnny looks away to the mountains, and I get the feeling he wishes he could just get on to other business but he's got to help me first.

"Son, ain't nothing I want from you, ain't nothing you could give me. I'm just here to give you a chance to get faith, based on the twelve-year-old boy you once were."

I look at him a long time, blinking hard, trying to make him vanish. But he doesn't.

I look at the river and the falls, and I look back at Johnny. He says, "Boy, I'd be much obliged if you'd decide one way or the other. June's waitin' on me."

I see how purple the mountains are, and how the rolling hills cast deep, green shadows, and how exquisitely still the red cows look as they graze, and I just want to cry, just cry, my heart broken with how good it all is.

Next minute, I'm standing there with my toes over the edge and my arms out at my sides and it's like this: I can walk away and die, or I can jump and die . . . or maybe, live. In a different way, but better maybe . . . I'm not really thinking that clearly.

I'm standing there with my toes over the edge and my arms out at my sides and I'm hearing a car coming—no, two cars.

I can walk away, but I know that if there's no God and no faith, there's nothing I want to live for. And if there is, if he can pick me up and float me across this river, well, then life is whatever it is meant to be, and I'll find out what that is and I'll just be doing what I'm supposed to be doing. And I know I'd better hurry if I'm going to do it because there are tourists pouring out of those cars. . . .

So . . . "Lord, float me on over. . . ."

I jump.

They wrote about me in the papers. You'll find the articles in that old album I keep in the bottom of my dresser.

Witnesses said how I got too close to the edge and fell into the water, how I was swept under a few times and then popped up in a quiet pool on the other side, how I dragged myself out and miraculously had no injuries and walked away from the whole thing. Local TV stations wanted to interview the survivor, but he declined. Instead they talked about the other people that had fallen in from time to time and died.

This is what I tell you, son.

Johnny was gone by the time I thought to look for him. The ambulance took me away after that. I would have said to him, "I thought God was going to float me over," and he would have said, "You didn't specify float by air or by water."

I wouldn't have argued with him.

Besides, it felt like I was floated. I was light as a leaf landing on the water. The water was warm, and I felt this giant hand pushing me under and then pulling me out again. I lay on that big rock in the sunshine and I tell you, son, I bawled like a baby I was so happy.

Life's been good since then. I got married to a nice girl, don't you think? Best mother a kid could want, you've said so yourself. I went to work every day and came home every day and took pride in my shelter, in my own little corner of the world God gave me. And your mom, she loved me with her wise cooking ways. No one would look at me and say, Now there goes a man who got a miracle. They might not even be able to tell I've got faith.

But I do.

Son, you know I do.

Sure, there's been some pretty scary legends built up around God, but that's not his fault. If it looks like a Johnny Cash and it talks like a Johnny Cash and it sings like one—well, most likely you've got one.

I'm taking the Juice out of my arm now, son. I know you love me enough not to stop me. Listen, son. I love you. It's all right. . . . It's so easy. . . . It's all right.

Ah.

Son, I've never loved you so much as I do now.

There's been times I had to move mountains in my life. Like when your sister was born premature and the doctors said she couldn't live. I said to God, Sir, you know I've got faith. And sure enough he delivered us. He didn't float me over that one either. We had to cross the hard way, day after day, until one day we took her home and Lord, she's been one beautiful kid.

He's not going to float me over this one, either. But son, I can feel his giant hand. And I'm looking forward to seeing Johnny and June, and as a matter of fact, there's a white Cadillac out my front door right now, and I'm feeling my faith coming on. . . .

Ah.

X X X X X

Born in Taber, Alberta, Martine Leavitt is the author of six novels for young adults: The Dragon's Tapestry *(1992),* The Prism Moon *(1993),* The Taker's Key *(1998),* The Dollmage *(2001),* Tom Finder *(2003)— all published by Red Deer Press—and, most recently,* Heck Superhero *(2004) published by Red Deer and Front Street Books in the U.S.. Leavitt has an Honors BA from the University of Calgary and an MFA from Vermont College, and works full time as a copy editor. The creative project she is most proud of, however, are her seven children and three grandchildren, all of whom have been critically acclaimed.*

THE THINGS YOU SEE IN MOVIES

Diana Aspin

ranny had been out all night and hadn't called home. She and her best friend, Lana, had watched horror movies, sucking on popcorn and swilling beers. Her head ached and the sun seemed like a car headlight, only a million times brighter. She shook the front door. She kicked it. Her parents had locked her out! Ankle deep in fresh snow, she shielded her eyes and peered up at her bedroom.

Yes! The window she'd crawled out of the night before was still open. She scrambled up the old maple, raised it, and bellied in. She cursed at the drapes; she was certain *she* hadn't closed them. Franny flopped onto her neatly made bed—tidy mothers!—and closed her eyes. Like some surreal movie, the intense light from outside still blazed across the inside of her eyelids. She was dropping off to sleep when a noise woke her.

Franny strained to hear but all she discerned was the boom-boom-boom of blood pumping through her ears. No. There it was again! From the kitchen—a shuffling noise.

"Dad!" she shouted. "Mom!" Come to think of it, she would have heard their voices. She shot bolt upright. "Mom?" This time more whimper than shout. Franny twisted the wet hem of her jeans.

If it wasn't her parents, who was it?

What was it? As though in reply, another shuffle. A leper's feet gliding across the kitchen linoleum. Something being dragged. Be serious, she told herself. Lepers? She should never have watched those horror movies.

Suddenly Franny's eyes flew wide open. Of course! It was their dog, Tessa, drifting from room to room the way she did when she was left alone.

"Tess! Tess girl!"

Franny tiptoed into the hallway. It was gloomy and cold; the heat was turned down. Someone had drawn the bedroom drapes. The hairs on her forearms rose, her tummy tightened.

Keep calm.

Breathe.

She breathed in—and remembered the movies. The things you see in horror movies stay with you forever. Those grisly specifics: a shotgun blast that leaves an eyeball embedded in a blood-splattered wall; a killer's chewed-up ear; a bare window reflecting only a cozy, well-lit room. While outside the window, lurking, stalking—who knows what? They'd taken turns scaring each other too. Lana's head in a noose, slumped to one side, tongue lolling, eyes alarmingly vacant. Franny, jaws slack, eyes rolled back, pretending to swivel her head around like in *Poltergeist*.

Get a grip! Now! Franny kicked open the door of her parents' room.

Boy, was it dark. And was it ever neat. Usually her mom's clothes were tossed onto the chair by the window, books piled higgledy-piggledy on her bedside table. It was tidier than when they were on vacation, or when company was coming. As far as Franny knew, neither of those things were about to happen. Two brave tugs at the drapes and light tumbled in. A low, menacing growl made Franny start.

"Tess!" Their black Labrador retriever crouched in the corner of the room, eyes huge, teeth bared. "Here, girl." Tess froze, brown eyes fixed straight ahead. The dog's fear was palpable; Franny's knees buckled.

She slid down the wall by the window, hugged her knees to her chest. "You heard it too, Tess, didn't you." It wasn't a question. There was no doubt in her mind the dog *knew* they weren't alone.

"There's a reasonable explanation," Franny whispered into her cupped hands. An antiseptic smell, one she knew but couldn't place, rode her warm breath. "There has to be. *Has* to be."

It wasn't just the noises that freaked her out.

It was the dark house.

The unusual cold.

The dog's behavior.

The locked door. They'd never, ever locked her out. No matter what she'd done. She sniffed. That clinical smell. Maybe the soap she'd used at Lana's.

The shuffling noise started up again. Franny gripped the collar of her sweatshirt. She buried her nose in it. *Black Christmas.* The very name of the movie and her insides plummeted. The movie was set on the U of T campus. Police guarded this student house. Cops everywhere but where the killer was.

Inside the house.

Inside it. Making phone calls. Worst of all, upstairs in a narrow attic window, known only to the viewer, a body shrouded in cloudy plastic, rope pulled tight around its neck, rocked ghoulishly, rhythmically, backward and forward.

Franny held her breath. The shuffling had stopped. Yet her every fiber pulsed along with her heart. She ached to pee. Then . . . another noise! A click-click. Followed by silence. Click-click. Franny saw them in her mind's eye: disembodied fingers, nails against a window pane.

Tess's dark lips reared slowly from her teeth. "It's only . . ." Franny began, but her tongue jammed to her palate.

Franny worked saliva into her mouth. She swallowed hard. "You're a guard dog, Tess," she hissed. "Act like one!" Some deep part of her began to vibrate.

Click-click. Click-click. Her chin quivered. She knew it was either march down there or die of fright. She rose. Put one foot in front of the other until she was in the hallway.

She gripped the oak railing like it was the handle of an ax.

Began her descent.

It was dark downstairs too, kitchen blinds pulled against the midday sun. On the counter sat their giant coffee percolator and beside it a row of cups and saucers. Of course! It was Saturday. Her dad's garden club meeting. The members took turns hosting it. Her mom had made sandwiches and a fruit cake.

But before she could ask herself where her parents were, she heard a shuffle. She froze. Turned to face it. In the corner of the kitchen, a heap of plastic her dad had used while wallpapering shifted in the breeze from the open window.

Another click-click. Franny followed the sound.

"Oh! Is *that* all!" The blinds, hoisted by the wind, slammed against the window frame. Click. Slammed again. Click.

"You're such a fool, Franny!" She raised the blinds.

She staggered back. It was as though the sun had inched closer to Earth. Its light so potent it seemed to burn through to her sockets.

Perhaps she was a vampire! She laughed so loud and long she had to sit down and catch her breath. Wait until she told Lana about all this. She grabbed the cordless phone and stabbed in Lana's number.

Come on. Come on. Get up, Lana. I know you're there.

But Lana was lazy. She wasn't getting out of bed. That, or she was still as comatose as she was when Franny left her. Well, mystery solved. She'd shower and change before her parents came home.

As she showered, Franny thought about horror movies. How once you watched them every click, bang, and whisper in a house freaked you out. You could go psycho just thinking about it. *Psycho.* Idiot! Why did she say that?

Reluctantly, Franny tipped her head back under the stream of pulsating water. She groped for the shampoo bottle. Her hands folded around something limp and slimy.

"Aaaaa-ah!" Franny dropped it. Blinked down. It was a decomposing sponge, gelatinous and green with mold. Franny, angry at herself, kicked it against the wall. She closed her eyes and let the water hammer against her skull, blocking out all sound.

As Franny turned off the shower, she heard the front door bang. At last. They were home!

Relieved, Franny watched rivulets of water meet and part as they raced down the steamed-up shower door. Then Tess growled. The low, long growl ran across the surface of Franny's skin like electricity. Despite the heat, an icy wave swept from her head to her feet. Then Tess whimpered and through the steamed-up shower door Franny saw it.

Someone—or some *thing*—gliding about the bedroom. Franny felt her innards shift. Impossible though it seemed, the wet hair in the nape of her neck stiffened. Cannibals and zombies, lepers and ax murderers. None of these could elicit her unadulterated terror.

For Franny knew—knew at a visceral level—it was not her mom who'd come in.

Her mom would have called out. It was not her dad either. There were no heavy footfalls, only an incalculable silence. The high-pitched, rhythmic screech of the *Psycho* soundtrack began to play inside Franny's skull.

She saw the raised knife.

Norman Bates's face. Those lights-are-on-but-there's-no-one-home, crazed eyes of his.

Franny pinned herself to the shower wall.

Go away! Go away! Ple-eeeeeease go away!

A river of steaming urine meandered down her thighs. She sank to the shower floor. Lay flat. Belly against the warm, wet tiles, invisible. Tess yelped, as though she'd been hurt.

She imagined her parents finding their daughter in a pool of blood, throat slit ear to ear. Finding Tess, entrails wormed across the rug, lips drawn back in an eternity of terror. She was about to cry out, "Come and get me. Get it over with!" when she heard her mom's voice.

"Lana, is that you?"

"Yes!" Franny cried. "It's me!" A humongous sob burst from her.

Oh, thank you God! Thank you. Thank you. I will never never stay out all night again. No more horror movies.

Naked, she scrambled on her hands and knees into the bedroom. There was no one there.

She grabbed a towel from the linen closet and clutched it to her. "Mom?"

There was no one in the hallway either. A ribbon of light bordered the bathroom door. Someone was in there. Perhaps one of her dad's garden club buddies.

Franny slid back into her skin.

Never again.

Never.

Half crying, half giggling, she wrapped the towel around herself and headed downstairs.

She sat down heavily on the fourth step up. Her mom's words boomeranged back.

Lana, are you there?

Lana? Why would her mom be asking if *Lana* was there? Franny had left Lana in bed with a hangover. While Franny stared at the flowered glass door of the grandfather clock in the hallway, her mom appeared.

Opening the door of the old clock, her mom pushed the golden fingers until they told the correct time.

"Mom?"

The clock door clicked shut. Her mom lay her cheek against it. "Mom? What's wrong?"

Her mom spidered her arms up the door until they were above her, palms flat against the glass. Then she slid to her knees.

A voice behind her made Franny jump. "Don't cry, Mrs. Carlson."

Lana!

Franny spun around. It had been Lana in the bedroom! She looked nothing like this morning: red-eyed, wild-haired, popcorn clinging to her sweater. She wore a simple, black skirt and sweater, black panty hose and shoes.

"Lana!" Franny exclaimed. "What are *you* doing here?"

Lana ignored her. "It's not anyone's fault, Mrs. Carlson," she said. "The car got stuck on the tracks. She couldn't get out."

"What car? Who?" Franny asked. "Is anyone going to let me in on this? Or am I going to sit here until I catch my death?"

Lana helped Franny's mother to her feet.

What am I?! Chopped liver! Angrily, Franny pulled the towel more tightly around herself. "Lana!" she snapped. Lana was pissing her off royally.

"Lana! Are you deaf or what?!"

Tess bolted down the stairs and into the kitchen. "Tess?" her mom said.

Lana glanced up the stairs. Franny bulged her eyes. She stuck out her tongue. She pretended to rotate her head. Lana turned away and hugged Franny's mom.

"Lana!" Franny screamed. "Look at me!"

The railings glided by. Then the top of the stairs. Then the wall.

To Franny's horror—*My God! My God*—her head revolves, steadily, like the hands of a clock. Franny closes her eyes tight to keep from being dizzy. The movement stirs the smell of her hands and she remembers what the smell was. Dissecting frogs at school. Formaldehyde! *Who* couldn't get out of the car? *Who* was dead? Formaldehyde? The blinding light again. Like car headlights, only bigger and brighter. Like the sun inching its way toward Earth. Like the end of the world. She sees Lana and her mother float by. The railings. The top of the stairs. The wall.

She hears screaming. Her own.

And the sound of a train—*a train*—bearing down on her.

X X X X X

Diana Aspin was born in Blackpool, England. Her first book, Ordinary Miracles *(Red Deer Press), was published in 2003. Her short story, "Mom," won a Thistledown Press competition and was published in* Opening Tricks *(1998). Her story, "Deep Freeze," was a runner-up in another Thistledown competition and was published in* Notes Across the Aisle *(1995). She has placed third in the Toronto Star Short Story competition and has been a runner-up twice. Diana taught short story writing and freefall writing to adults from 1995–2001. She has worked as a waitress, sales assistant, civil servant, office cleaner, cinema usherette, stay-at-home mom, and counselor in a women's shelter.*

The Night the Rabbit Died

Alice Walsh

There are thirteen at the dinner table, counting Judd. Elsie did not expect Judd to be here, and she feels uneasy with him watching her from across the table.

"I don't know what Aunt Faye was thinking," she said to her cousin Leah, just before they sat down to eat. "Inviting *him* here for Christmas."

"He's different since your mother died," Leah tried to reassure her. "Don't drink nearly so much as he used to. Besides, he *is* Maddie's father."

Judd was the reason Elsie left home when she was fifteen. Yet, in the two years she's been away, she's never really been free of him. She still awakes from dreams that leave her filled with anxiety, thinking of Judd and blood and dead animals. Although she never remembers the dreams, there is always an ominous awareness that lingers at the edge of her consciousness, just out of reach of her memory.

She shifts uneasily, knowing Judd's eyes are on her. A sly smile spreads across his whiskered face—a predatory smile.

"I feels right blessed having so many of yous here for Christmas," Aunt Faye says. She looks around the table at her children, some with spouses and children of their own. There's Christmas music on the stereo and, through the window behind her, snow is falling heavily. Maddie, Elsie's younger sister who moved in with their aunt after their mother died, is sitting next to Judd. Elsie realizes that she is unusually quiet this evening. "Some glad *you* could make it, Elsie," Aunt Faye says. "But my, how the time flies. Seems like only yesterday, sure, when you and Leah was playing with dolls."

Elsie gives her aunt a sad half-smile. Judd is still watching, sneering now, his big hand clumsily twirling the stem of a wineglass. Elsie averts her eyes, trying not to look at his hands—hands, he bragged, that could skin a rabbit in less than a minute. Elsie used to watch him peeling off their skins as easily as one peeled off a glove. She squirms, remembering how he would unceremoniously yank out the guts, heart, and kidneys, blood running down his arms, dripping bright red on the kitchen floor. He saved the paws to nail to the walls of his fishing shack, claiming they brought him good luck.

"How come you never skins the hands and feet?" Elsie once dared to ask.

He threw back his head and laughed, then pushed her roughly across the kitchen floor.

For anyone who cared to listen, Judd had a story to tell about each of his rabbits. "This feller was still alive when I come across him in the snare," he would say, holding up the dead rabbit by the scruff of the neck. "Had to give him a good jesus whack on the head to show him who was boss. And this sucker here chewed half his leg off, trying to get away. And looka this one. Weasels musta got at he. Look how the one ear is chewed off."

Once he brought home a live rabbit. Elsie and Maddie had played with it all afternoon, and Elsie had been hoping to keep it as a pet. That evening, though, Judd snatched the rabbit by the hind legs from its hiding place behind the stove. He cursed and swore as it squealed and wriggled to get free. Elsie watched, horrified, as he picked up the poker and brought it down on the rabbit's head. The rabbit stopped squealing, its legs stiffening in midair.

"More wine?" Aunt Faye asks, jolting Elsie back to the present. "My, you was an odd little youngster," she says as she refills Elsie's glass. "We never thought you'd outgrow your queer ways. Sure, I remembers all the times you'd come and stay with us." She chuckles. "I remembers how obsessed you used to be about rabbits."

Memories stir. Elsie had often been sent here as a young child when her mother was too sick to take care of her. Uncle Ned was alive then. And Gram. She can still picture Gram in her rocking chair by the stove, gnarled hands clutching her rosary.

"I seen a rabbit that was skinned, but it was still alive," Elsie once told her cousins, causing gales of laughter around the kitchen table.

"How could it be alive if it was skinned?" scoffed Tim, the oldest cousin.

"I knows what I seen," Elsie said stubbornly. "It had hands too."

"You means paws, my love," Aunt Faye said.

"No, the rabbit I seen had hands," Elsie insisted.

"Now don't you be tellin' them lies," said the old woman from her rocker. "You'd be better off sayin' yer prayers."

"It had arms and legs and feet too."

"Lies," said Gram. "Wait till you makes yer first confession; the priest'll fix you. You'll go straight to hell if you keeps on tellin' them lies."

Elsie felt her stomach grow cold. She hated it when Gram warned about hell. Everybody knew that old Lucy Barnes was in hell for eating meat on Friday. And Aunt Aggie would surely go to hell for marrying a Protestant. Father O'Brien once said that to marry a Protestant was a sin every bit as serious as robbery or murder. Gram allowed it was worse than that, and she vowed never to darken her sister's door again.

It was Judd who usually picked Elsie up at her aunt and uncle's house. She never wanted to go home and often cried, clinging to her aunt's skirt. Aunt Faye would promise that, in a day or so, she would go get her and bring her back for another visit. "What a hard ticket that one is," she once heard her aunt tell Judd as Elsie searched for her mitts. Laughing, she repeated what Elsie had told them about the rabbit. "You never knows what's goin' to come out of her next."

As soon as the door closed behind them, Judd grabbed Elsie's arm. "Keep yer damn trap shut, hear." He shook her hard. "If you goes around sayin' stuff like that, they'll be cartin' ye off to the Mental like poor old Nellie Newcomb." He twisted Elsie's arm until she cried out in pain. "And if ever I hears tell of you spreadin' lies like that again, I'll knock yer damn head off."

Elsie tried to get away, but Judd encircled her neck with his arm. "They'll be lockin' you up for sure," he hissed.

When he finally let go of her, Elsie fled across the field and into the woods, the white tassel on her cap bobbing as she ran through the deep snowdrifts. Snow got inside her boots and clung to her dress, but still she kept running, her skinny little legs in their white leotards moving as fast as they could away from Judd.

As time went by, Elsie began to wonder if she had really seen the strange rabbit, or if she had only imagined it. Was she starting to go mental like poor Nellie? Nellie Newcomb, as everyone in Calvert's Cove knew, had been sent away because she told her mother the priest had put his hand under her skirt when she was leaving the confession box. "Now you knows a Catholic priest wouldn't do the likes of that," Elsie had heard Gram say more than once. "Sure, when people gets low-minded like Nellie, they're liable to say anything."

Whenever she thought of Nellie, Elsie imagined her locked in a wire-mesh cage with barely enough room to stand up. The image filled her with fear, and she decided never to speak of the strange rabbit again. Only crazy people saw things that other people didn't. Unless, of course, it was the Virgin Mary you saw. Daisy May Murphy claimed to have seen the Blessed Virgin, and the bishop made a special trip all the way from Corner Brook. Told Daisy May's mother that if Daisy May had any more visions, he would contact the pope and they would consider preparing her for sainthood.

"Sainthood, me arse," Uncle Ned said when he heard the news. But no one dared call Daisy May crazy.

Elsie tried hard to forget about the rabbit. She pushed it to the back of her mind, the way one might push an unwanted piece of clothing to the back of a closet. Whenever it tugged at the edge of her memory, she would stuff it back a little farther until, eventually, it became as obscure as a dream.

✗ ✗ ✗ ✗ ✗

But now, sitting in her aunt's house on this Christmas Eve, memories of the rabbit crawl into her mind like a cancer sneaking out of remission. She glances nervously at Judd, fear knotting her stomach. He pulls back his thin lips in a leer, revealing yellowish teeth, black at the gum line. A glimmer of memory surfaces in Elsie's mind. The wineglass slips from her hand, clattering noisily to the table. She watches as the red wine seeps into the tablecloth like blood.

"Are you okay, Elsie?" Aunt Faye asks anxiously.

Elsie is aware that everyone is staring. The room swirls, and she grips the arms of the chair for support as more memories rise to the surface.

✗ ✗ ✗ ✗ ✗

It was another Christmas Eve, nearly ten years earlier, when Elsie awoke to the sound of her mother screaming. At first, she thought Judd was beating her again. But Judd had sounded frightened. Elsie had never known him to be afraid of anything. "Holy Christ," he was yelling. "Whas I s'pose t' do now?"

Elsie figured he was drunk. She wanted to go to her mother, but her mother had warned her—made her promise, even—to stay out of Judd's way when he was drinking.

Alice Walsh   107

She got out of bed, taking care not to wake Maddie, who was asleep beside her. Opening the flimsy curtain that divided her bedroom from the kitchen, Elsie padded across the cold floor in her bare feet. The kerosene lamp on the table had the wick turned down low, casting a pale, eerie glow. She stood by the window, shivering in her threadbare nightgown. Rubbing a patch of frost from the small, square window, she peered out into the dark night. Across the road, the Murphys had colored Christmas lights in their window that twinkled on and off. Almost everyone in Calvert's Cove had electricity now, and a lot of people had decorated their trees and windows with lights. The Prichets, farther down in the cove, even had lights put on a tree in their yard.

Crouching down in the space between the stove and the rocker, Elsie drew her knees up to her chin. The tiny house was filled with her mother's moans. Out on the road, she could hear voices. People were leaving to go to midnight Mass. If Mama was feeling better tomorrow, maybe she would take them to church. Last Christmas, she got to hold the Baby Jesus that was in the manger on the altar. Maybe Father O'Brien would tell that story again about how Joseph and Mary came into Bethlehem looking for a place for Jesus to be born. She enjoyed the story, except the part about a bad man named Herod who went around trying to kill all the babies.

She could hear more voices outside. The Murphys were leaving to go to church. Since Daisy May had her vision, her mother took her to church often. "I hopes Sandy Claws comes and brings you all kinds of good stuff." Elsie recognized the voice of Bert Saunders who lived up on the hill.

"I hopes he brings me a dollie," said Daisy May. "Like the one I seen in Howard Farrell's store window. Cries like a real baby, wets her diaper and everyt'ing."

Elsie wondered if Sandy Claws would come to her this year. Her mother had been so sick, she hadn't even bothered to put up a tree. She knew Aunt Faye would come by with a Christmas box. She always brought apples and oranges, and sometimes mitts and vamps for Elsie and Maddie. Elsie knew she couldn't always depend on Sandy Claws, but she could always count on Aunt Faye.

Outside, she could hear the crunch of winter boots on the frozen snow. There were more voices and laughter. Somewhere, a barn door banged shut. Old Mike Pelly was singing, "Silent night, holy night," his voice slurring in and out of tune. From the bedroom, Elsie's mother groaned like a wounded animal, her breath coming in short little pants.

✗ ✗ ✗ ✗ ✗

"Are you okay, Elsie?" Aunt Faye asks again, bringing Elsie's thoughts back to the present. She is still dizzy, still reeling in shock from the rush of memory. Images she had banished from her mind as a young child hit her with a whole new impact. The truth lies before her now with startling clarity. Why couldn't she have seen it before? She looks at her aunt. Hadn't she known—hadn't any of them known? Had her own mother gone to her grave without knowing how evil Judd really was?

Elsie holds her head between her hands. The memories are coming hard and fast. She can't stop them, any more than she could stop her mother's screams on that Christmas Eve so long ago.

✗ ✗ ✗ ✗ ✗

The cries and moans had gone on for hours while Elsie crouched in the shadows, her hands over her ears in an attempt to drown it all out.

After a while, the cries ceased and there were hushed whispers and low, urgent voices. Judd came out of the bedroom, his shadow large and distorted on the kitchen wall. He was carrying the rabbit, holding it in front of him like an offering, the flame from the kerosene lamp radiating a rim of light around its head. Elsie saw that it had feet and toes. And hands too, tiny outstretched palms. It gave a soft little cry, and she knew it was alive.

Judd crossed the room and picked up the poker.

X X X X X

Alice Walsh grew up in northern Newfoundland and now lives in Lower Sackville, Nova Scotia, with her husband and two daughters. She graduated from St. Mary's University with a degree in English and Criminology, and from Acadia with a master's degree in children's literature. She writes fiction and non-fiction for adults and children, and her published work includes three children's books: Something's Wrong with Kayla's Mother *(Nimbus, 1992);* Uncle Farley's False Teeth *(Annick, 1998); and* Heroes of Isle aux Morts *(Tundra, 2001). A fourth book,* Pomiuk; Prince of the North, *will be released in 2004 by Beach Holme.*

Hunting Snakes

W.D. Valgardson

When I was a kid we used to go up to my father's fish camp. The road, when dry, was covered in crushed limestone and the dust was so thick that when other cars passed we rolled the windows up tightly and held our breaths. Sometimes we had to stop until the dust drifted off into the tamarack forest. By the time we reached the camp, our hair was stiff with dust, and dust clogged our eyes and nostrils. Often, like bandits, we tied handkerchiefs to cover our noses and mouths.

When it was wet, the crushed limestone disappeared and great clay ruts appeared and filled with rain. The truck slipped and slid in the tracks and we didn't dare stop for fear that, once stopped, we could not get the truck free of the clay. Our goal, then, was to not slip from the road into the deep muskeg ditches filled with brown water and green slime. Trucks had slid into them, then sunk down through the soft muskeg before anyone could come to winch them out. Sometime in the distant future, archeologists would find vehicles and their loads from an ancient civilization and celebrate.

None of this ever stopped us from going any time my father asked us. Our friends even vied for extra space in the car my mother drove.

There was, my father said, freedom beyond the paved road, freedom as we drove deeper and deeper, away from the few scattered Mennonite farms into thick, dark forest. We left behind the yards with their chickens for trees with hawks and ravens; the cows for moose charging, startled, from the bush. We left the telephone lines behind. He hadn't bought a satellite dish in those days, so we left TV behind too. Freedom, my father said as the truck slipped and slid in the loose gravel, trailing a great tail of white dust.

We turned in where a large spruce had been tipped over in a windstorm so that we now called it the dragon's head. The bush slapped at the sides of the truck, for the road now was just two worn tracks with grass growing between. Finally, we broke into the open and could see the lake. There was freedom.

On the first trip in the spring of that year, the grass in the cleared area around the buildings had grown waist-high. The snow still hunched in the deep shade, hard, crystalline, resentful. The moose maple had sprung up like weeds, and the winter storms had tossed about branches and pulled shingles off the sheds. All the tin cans and paper that had been thrown out during the winter now lay scattered on the sodden ground.

We drove through the grass, pulled up short where the land sloped down to a shingle beach. And then we spilled out of the car and truck, yelling and running and twirling, as if we'd reached the promised land.

My father cleared a bird's nest from the chimney, and my mother started the cookstove to make tea to go with the pie and cake she'd brought. The first taste of canned milk was like a memory unlocked of a past life where there was no school, no sitting for endless hours in rows, listening to someone drone on about math or English.

"Bears," my younger brother yelled. We all went to look. There were deep claw marks on the icehouse wall.

"The smell from the meat in the sawdust and the ice," my father explained.

There was no meat, but its smell was still thick in the dark, insulated confines of the icehouse. The bear had ripped repeatedly at the planks, tearing long gashes. I ran my finger down the row of splinters, imagined what those claws could do to my body. Bears, we knew, lurked on the edges of the forest, sniffing, watching, bold enough to sometimes come into the garden to lick away the ripe strawberries.

My brother, Dale, is two years younger than I am, and it is my job to look after him. It shouldn't be hard, but he has a way of slipping out of sight. One moment he's there—I glance at something, I glance back—and he is gone. There are wolves lying in the thick, tangled darkness of the forest, their yellow eyes watching. We see their tracks in the morning, large paw prints going down to the water's edge. There are some lynx, but they are so shy it is a miracle to see one, and the moose are so big it is impossible not to see them. Once one attacked our car, charging head down, determined to keep the road to himself.

My father says the real dangers are the ones you can't see. The quicksand, the undertow beneath a calm surface that sucks swimmers down and holds them against the bottom, the thin ice. Danger is all around us, all the time.

There are a lot of snakes, and that is where my brother has gone. I find him searching among the large cracks in the limestone cliffs along the shore. Water gets into cracks, freezes, and slowly, remorselessly, silently, pushes the layered cliffs apart. It seems impossible. Solid limestone cracked open, the resulting crevices leading deeper and deeper into the cliffs. You can walk right into them. They're full of shadows and ice. Sometimes there's still ice in them in the middle of summer. The air is thick and stale. Farther north along the road, there is a place where the crevices lead to caves, but few people have been in them because a sudden northeast wind will send water pouring into some of them. Others have bats. Bats eat mosquitoes but my mother says they carry rabies, and if they bite or scratch you, you foam at the mouth and run in circles, then die. Sometimes, when we're visiting at Pine Dock, we hear other stories about the caves, about strange people with yellow skin and pointed teeth who some locals claim to have seen. There are stories, old stories, passed from the Cree to the trappers and hunters, and from them to the people who now live in the area. Stories of Wendigo, yellow-skinned women who are cannibals, who scavenge the shoreline for dead fish or animals, who steal the bodies of the drowned. That is why there is such a determined search when a boat founders or a swimmer disappears.

"It's too early," I say. Later when the sun warms the rock, hundreds of garter snakes will appear, slithering out of the holes, sunning themselves on the rocks, and Dale will cheerfully pick them up and sling them around his neck, wearing them like necklaces. He'll stuff them inside his shirt where they'll curl around his warm body. "Besides, you're not supposed to be in here."

Three years before, he'd gone snake hunting, edging deeper and deeper into a crevasse, following a large snake, maybe six feet long, squeezing farther in as the sides narrowed. I'd lost him that time. The crevasses are like a maze, sometimes open from the top, sometimes covered in moss and forest-floor debris so there is only the faintest reflected light. I'd been searching in one and then another, when I heard him yelling. The sound echoes and re-echoes in those narrow cuts, so it is hard to tell where it comes from. I left one crevasse, plunged into another, backed out, plunged into a third. The rock was loose underneath and the edges of the walls were sharp, so I kept slipping and banging into the points of rock. The walls narrowed until I was edging in sideways. I slipped off my jacket since it kept snagging on the rock. I don't like narrow, confined places and I wanted to leave him, to rush back, calling for my father, but he or my mother couldn't have done anything because they were both bigger than I was.

I wiggled between the walls until I was able to reach out and grab his hand. He was crying and calling my name, "Bobby, Bobby," something he hadn't done since he was little and had nightmares. He was flat between the walls, with one arm out toward me and one arm reaching into the darkness.

"I'm here," I said. "Stop blubbering."

"It's got me," he said. "It won't let go. I'm pulling as hard as I can."

"The snake!" I said.

"I don't know. Something. It's got my hand."

There were some shafts of light where the moss cover was broken. I bent down, picked up a rock, and threw it up. It made a hole, then clattered back. I threw three more. The light was pale and thin, and I couldn't see anything beyond Dale because he blocked the narrowing crevasse.

He loved to create dramatic situations. Once he pretended that he was being dragged down into the water. We all plunged in to rescue him. Another time he claimed he was being chased by a great white owl. He was a kid with an imagination. I loosened my grip on his hand but immediately felt him being tugged away from me. I tightened my grip again.

"Don't let go," he screamed.

I pulled back, but he was stuck firm. I edged closer. Bone-rack, bone-rack, he'd sometimes tease me, trying to get me to chase him. Now my being a bone-rack was all that let me get this close. I looked back the way I had come. The line was straight and I could see the blue of the lake, the paler sky, the shafts of light along the crevasse. One of the holes in the moss above let down a shaft of light that played on the left side of Dale's face. Tears streamed down it. The other side was in darkness.

"Pull, Bobby," he cried. I dug my feet into the shale and pulled as hard as I could. "I love you," he said.

I nearly lost my grip. He never said he loved anybody. Not me, not Mom, not Dad. He never even said he loved Lassie, our collie.

He was, my father had said, a little devil. Tormenting and teasing, doing things he shouldn't and then clenching his jaw and defying any of us to do anything about it.

I pulled harder and felt him edge toward me. "Nothing—nothing's going to get you," I said through clenched teeth. I pulled and pulled, and then he came free so suddenly that I slid backward, scraping the back of my head and banging my knees.

I held his hand tight. We wiggled and squirmed toward the opening. When we were back on the shore, he held up his right arm. His jacket had torn loose at the shoulder, the sleeve gone. He started to laugh, high-pitched, hysterical, throwing his head back, waving his arm around. "My jacket was caught, that was all," he said. "My jacket. It was just my jacket." Then he started to cry, and I put my arms around him. Maybe his jacket was just snagged on a sharp piece of rock, but there were hard red marks on his hand, as if something coarse had gripped it tight.

My father was scything grass. He'd been expecting us to help him by raking it and piling it up on the shore for burning. He was singing at the top of his voice while he worked. At the top of his voice. He stopped scything, tipped the scythe blade up, took the sharpening stone out of his pocket, and ran it quickly back and forth along the blade.

"What happened?" my mother asked. She was looking at where the jacket sleeve was missing.

"He got caught on some rocks while chasing snakes," I explained.

My father was scything again. "Freedom, freedom," he was singing, making up his own song. My mother just shook her head in disgust. Lucky it was an old jacket.

We raked grass in the sunlight and drank the lemonade my mother made from fresh lemons and lake water. It was too early for swimming but, with blankets wrapped around us, we had a bonfire on the beach and roasted wieners for hot dogs, and heated up beans in a can.

Later in the summer, on our third trip, I think, I took a flashlight and went back into the crevasse. I took a gaff as well. I reached up with the gaff and broke away the moss covering so that it rained down onto me. My noisy slipping in the shale and the falling of the pieces of moss scared away the snakes. They wiggled out of sight into cracks and holes. I broke moss all the way back to where I'd held Dale's hand, then I went back out, climbed up to the forest floor and following the opening I'd made, knocked more moss down, but the crevasse quickly narrowed at the top until you could only get a straw through. I used the flashlight, probing to see if I could find the sleeve and snag it with the gaff but I couldn't find it. It could, of course, have been dragged away by any number of small animals to make a nest.

We're older now. We still come to the fish camp, but now we are inclined to sit around the campfire and ask questions, rather than just sing songs about someone coming around a mountain. "What's freedom?" was one question I asked my father.

"Being able to choose," he replied. But I wasn't sure if he meant the freedom to choose to come to the camp, to not have a telephone, to not have television, to not have to go to the barbershop every day in the off-season. Or something else.

We were all choosing, of course. All the time. I was choosing to study, to think about going to university, to do my homework, to work delivering groceries. My mother was choosing to keep the house clean, to make meals, to go back to work part-time, to not get involved with the Ladies Aid this year.

And Dale was choosing—but I wasn't sure what. He'd never again said that he loved me. But he'd quit tormenting me. Around me, he just smiled and put his head down, or looked sideways at me out of the corners of his eyes. I sometimes managed to get him to do homework with me, go to a movie, or play catch, but he wasn't into organized sports. He didn't join a curling or baseball team. He was choosing to hang around the pool hall, slipping in the back door because he was too young to be there; choosing to hide his cigarettes under the neighbor's cottage; choosing to hang out with a group who spent their time doing something in one of the cabins that held gas boats, beached for the winter. The cabins were boarded up, and I wondered what they found to do in the darkness. Some people say they're a gang, but they're just a bunch of kids hanging around together.

The last few times we'd come out to the camp, Dale had managed to talk Mom and Dad into letting him stay at one of his friends'. The last time there'd been some drinking, some trouble at the school, a window broken, some vandalism; so this time the folks had insisted he come with us.

So here we are, just inside one of the crevasses, him looking into the darkness, peering this way and that to see if any of the snakes had come out early, him edging into the shadows, me standing at the edge of the sunlight, turning to look at the blue lake and pale, sun-filled sky behind us.

"It was just your jacket caught on a point of rock," I say.

"Yeah," he replies, but his voice is muffled because he's eased farther in, become less distinct in the shadows. I know he's afraid, but it's like he's got to see what's there. It's like the crazy stunt on his bike when he broke his leg. Or getting caught shoplifting a package of candy when he had ten dollars in his pocket.

And I wish that as he edges deeper into the crevice, I wish he'd say he loves me.

X X X X X

W. D. Valgardson was born in Winnipeg, lived in Gimli, Manitoba, then returned to Winnipeg to attend United College. Once he graduated, he began teaching high school in rural Manitoba. He earned a Bachelor of Education from the University of Manitoba and then a Master of Fine Arts from the University of Iowa. Oberon Press published his first book of short stories in

*1973. Since then he has had twelve more books pub-
lished, a dozen plays produced, and a number of movies
made from his novels and short stories.*

*He taught high school English and art for a num-
ber of years, then taught English and creative writing at
Cottey College in Missouri. In 1974 he joined the fac-
ulty at The University of Victoria and remained there,
teaching fiction workshops and theory courses, until his
retirement in 2004. His work has been awarded numer-
ous prizes and has been translated and published in
many different countries. He holds an honorary doctor-
ate from the University of Winnipeg and is a member of
The Royal Society of Canada.*

MY NAME IS KYRA

Kristyn Dunnion

*M*y name is Kyra. *I'm wearing my favorite jeans, three layers of my personally designed, hand-painted T-shirts, and my Castro-inspired Cuban resistance cap. I'm freestyling on my favorite skateboard near the shopping mall entrance, hanging with all my friends. I'm pulling flips, going fakey to the curb. I rip off a fast shoveit, so I'm still facing the same way, but my board spins around beneath my feet. I circle hard to the left to gather speed. I grit my teeth. I'm bearing down on the wide set of cement steps. I pop and jump. I'm up! I hit the handrail. I'm not sliding on my board; I'm skating, riding the rail downhill. Air rushes by me and through me and because of me. I'm flying. I pull a beautiful acid-drop off the end. I land that trick like I own it, and end with a stylish no-comply board flip. I am flashing the Grinning Girl Skull that I painted on the bottom. I bow to my friends, bow to their huge applause.*

"Ky-ra! Ky-ra!" they shout and stomp.

Alex, my best friend, wolf whistles, fingers in mouth, and skates down the wheelchair ramp to be the first to hug me. The others crowd in, slap my back, high-five, ruffle my hair. Then Miriam appears. Gorgeous, flamboyant

Auntie Miriam, wearing tight jeans, high-top sneakers, and an I Fought the Law and I Won! T-shirt. Miriam's hair is cropped short and dyed Crayola red. She smiles and waves. She's getting smaller.

Miriam's hair hasn't been like that for four or five years.

I say, "Wait!"

Miriam blows kisses, whispers, "I love you, Kyra, I knew you could do it," and she shrinkydinks until she's gone. So does Alex, so do the guys from school, and so does my beautiful board. I turn quickly, run circles around the empty concrete, swish my shoulder-length, sea-green dreads. I crink my neck looking for all my friends. I tug my textured locks, twirl them, put one in my mouth, and chew it lightly.

I am dreaming of my old life, back in Canada. The one that died as suddenly as Miriam.

✗ ✗ ✗ ✗ ✗

Kyra wakes with dull fear in her throat. She keeps her eyes shut. She bites her bottom lip, but the pretty hoop she used to wear is long gone. Her fingers search out the coveted dreads, but they, too, have vanished. She rubs her head, its choppy stubble and angry tufts spawned at irregular intervals. She is suffocating under the heavy, raw cotton sheets, tucked in on three sides. She pinches her skin through the tangly, worn nightdress.

Yep, I'm awake.

Awake in the never ending nightmare of her new life. She whispers a mantra, her new morning ritual. She tells herself the broken facts of her present situation; she clings to the withering strands of her true self.

My name is Kyra. I am fifteen years old. I am somewhere in the American Midwest. I am temporarily living with my estranged biological Father. He is diabolically insane. I have been here two nights. Soon I will find my things. Then I will escape.

She hears the inevitable creaking footsteps of her Father, heading toward her bedroom door. He pauses just outside.

She wants to die.

x x x x x

On her way to congregation school, Kyra shuffles slowly, eyes to the ground. She is a half-living, shallow-breathing zombie. She's wearing the same outfit as yesterday, as every day since her arrival, courtesy of her Father. She hates the itchy, wool stockings, too short for her athletic legs, so the crotch stretches and sags unbearably. The smelly foot parts sweat in ugly boots, while the sun glares down mercilessly. Her long slip is stained under the arms by some previous occupant, and a ridiculous, pilgrim-style dress hangs over top. It even has a bow around the waist! In this outfit, her shorn head makes her look like a cancer patient, nothing like the cute punk girls back home. There's even a sun-bleached bonnet, like from *Little House on the Prairie*, and she wears it outside. She has to.

Other girls, similarly dressed but with long, braided hair, walk her to school. Most are blondes with mealy-looking skin and light-blue eyes. Ghosty. They take the dirt path in pairs, talking quietly to one another, quoting bible verses or something from the scripture reading they'd had the night before. Creepy.

On her first day, Kyra tried desperately to connect with them, but was met with blank stares. She'd said, "Does anyone have an iPod?" Hers was locked away with all her CDs and she was suffering withdrawal big-time. And, "Don't you listen to music? Where are the computers? I'll download some hot tracks for you." The only thing those girls were good for was ratting Kyra out to her Bible-thumping Father. This dump was worse than the one in that horrible flick, *Footloose,* one Miriam made her watch during a retro eighties film weekend they hosted for their friends.

The thought of Miriam makes her bite down to keep from crying. The wave of homesickness hits her hard and she stops abruptly, presses her thumbs into her eye sockets to fight off another rising attack of panic. She hadn't even said goodbye. She was a minor, not permitted to identify the body after the car accident, so Miriam's best friend had done that. Miriam had wanted to be cremated, and so it was. But when Kyra's long-lost Father suddenly appeared to take custody, he refused to stay for the scattering of the ashes. Miriam's ashes. Kyra had fallen into a daze, a brokenhearted stupor. Nothing was real to her. She nodded to the adults in their kitchen, shook this man's hand limply, was pulled away from Miriam's friends, from her own, from Alex, who sobbed uncontrollably and had to be restrained when Kyra's stern Father motioned her toward the waiting taxi. She had no say.

Alice, her silent walking partner, nudges her softly. When Kyra looks up, she notices the girl's shining, dark eyes for the first time. She is the only other non-blonde in the village. Alice's face is soft but worried. Humane, possibly. Nice?

They keep walking and soon catch up with the others.

My name is Kyra. I'm fifteen. My Father is the little king of this born-again, backwater pit stop in the middle of America the Strange. How can we be related? Which distant relative contacted this zealot, and why did they let him take me? Last night I tried to leave, just the potato sack on my back: forget my passport, money, my stuff. But my door is bolted on the outside. Will someone back home try to find me? Where exactly am I? I have been here four nights.

There are more kids in her Canadian homeroom than in this entire school. Here they're all members of her Father's great congregation, all live nearby in rural squalor, all with the same washed-out eyes and bad skin. Listless.

"Are we the oldest girls?" Kyra asks Alice.

"In school, yes, bless His heart."

Kyra waits for her to continue, but that's it. "Well, where do they go?" she prods.

"Tutoring," whispers Alice and lowers her eyes.

Kyra feels gooseflesh ripple her arms. She swallows hard. Alice squeezes her eyes tight shut, then opens them wide. Wide with foresight and fear.

Each night after supper Kyra's Father scrapes back his chair, tosses his cloth napkin down onto the plate and goes outside for a while. Kyra is alone with his wife, an ugly woman with bulging eyes, an overbite, and perpetual frown.

"What will happen to me next year?" Kyra sneaks a peek at the older woman while scrubbing away at the cornmeal pot.

"Ours is not to question the future, bless His heart," Stepmother says.

Kyra grips the pot till her knuckles whiten. "I mean with school."

Her stepmother starts up with the drying towel. She presses her mouth into a straight line, like she's thinking something through hard, or doing math. She says softly, "You'll be getting tutored."

Kyra pulls the cloth out of her stepmother's hands until she raises her chin and their eyes lock.

"In marrying ways," she whispers. She looks terrified but continues, trance-like. "In womanly obligations. Then the men'll vie for ye and you'll be sent to live with one of them. The one what gives your Father the most in return. That's how it's done round hereabouts. But your Father, bless Him, has a certain path for you first."

Kyra's panic consumes her and she drops the cloth. There's no way she'd marry some stodgy farmer, some old man, at the age of sixteen! She must get out of here, out of this creepy little nightmare town. When she blinks back some self-control, she says, "Thank you, Stepmother," because she knows it was a risk to say even that much.

"Call me Mother, bless you. Your Father told me you haven't known one since you was knee-high." She shook her head. "They call her the Dark-Haired Devil round here. Heretic. For all that I'm a Christian woman and haven't been able to give him a single spawn."

My mother, The Devil Heretic!

Kyra nodded and excused herself from the kitchen, but couldn't bring herself to say that word. She had few memories of her own mother; she'd had Auntie Miriam as her legal guardian since kindergarten. Miriam answered some of the inevitable questions about Kyra's parents. Said her sister had been a traveler, an adventurous spirit who, somewhere along the line, met up with a bearded man she initially admired. Said they had irreconcilable differences. That one night she simply left. She fled with baby Kyra and made her way north by the moon. She fought the cancer that ravaged her body, but succumbed when Kyra was still a little kid. As for her Father, Kyra thought she'd eventually meet him, though Miriam didn't exactly encourage it.

Miriam said, "He's a pious creep, Kyra, love. I don't know what my sister was thinking, but at least we got you out of the deal!"

Pious? Try psychotic.

Instead of going to the windowless room where she sleeps, Kyra heads quietly to the main room of the cabin. She hardly breathes. What would happen if He caught her snooping? The room is pretty bare. There's a worn carpet in the middle of the floor, and three hard-backed chairs around a hearth that won't be lit until the first snowfall. There's the family Bible, of course, a hand-stitched quilt folded on the rocking chair, and a large wooden chest. Some of her stuff might be in there, but it's done up tight with a thick padlock.

She opens her Father's bedroom door. The back of her neck prickles, she hears that scary-movie music inside her head. It makes her edgy. There's a wooden dresser with a washbasin on top. No mirror. A double bed with pale sheets takes up most of the room. The top quilts are folded back over the foot of the bed, and Kyra can see that the sheets are oddly tailored. Halfway down the bed are two medium-sized holes cut out of the sheet, side by side, with dark double stitching around the edges, drawing your eye right to them.

Disgusting.

The floor creaks. She whirls around. Her stepmother stands tall, rigid with anger, and her face shows no hint of the earlier sympathy. She hisses, "Don't be snooping in your Father's room." Her hands, calloused from constant hard work, push Kyra away. "Take my warning. Be gone."

Kyra runs back through the sitting room and into her own. She closes the door, but can't lock it.

My name is Kyra. Every day we eat the same mush for breakfast, the same for lunch, and a potato-and-cornmeal mush for supper. Every night we go to the Meeting Place where Father pontificates on some Bible story. Then some ugly old geezer does a scripture reading. The freak girls line up and sing hymns. I don't. I mouth the words. Alex must know something's up. No emails, no texties; nothing. The only phone in the whole town is at the Meeting Place, and women aren't allowed except for the nightly reading. I am losing it. I have been here eight nights.

Congregation school lets out around three so everyone can rush home to their chores. Kyra hates this the most. Back in Toronto she'd have basketball practice or she'd hang with her friends, down in the core. She'd skateboard with Alex, pull balancing tricks, flips, and shove-its. She didn't know many girls as good on a board as she and Alex were. Today she is pitching manure with Alice instead.

"Why do girls have to learn this?" says Kyra.

Alice almost laughs. "Women know to do most everything, inside and outside the dwelling. Except the scriptures, of course, and handling guns and rifles. That'd be for the menfolk. The Lord smiles on us, bless His heart," she says, and keeps shoveling.

"What do you mean?" Kyra throws down her rusty tool and grabs Alice's shoulder. "We're prisoners here, Alice. Nobody's smiling. Not you or me and certainly not the Lord, *if* he exists!"

Alice gasps. She pulls away, shakes her head fiercely. "No, Kyra, don't say that. Please, just work. Don't make things harder!"

"This is insane. You really don't get it, do you?" Kyra gulps back hysteria. "People aren't like this in other places, you know. This is totally fucked."

Alice covers her ears and scrunches her eyes tight.

I said the F word.

"At least it's only manure." Alice rocks back and forth.

"I'm sorry," Kyra says.

Alice says, "Manure only smells strong. Never harmed me none, bless him."

My name is Kyra. I am smarter than all this. This is just a bad movie I rented for fun. All day I hunt clues. See miles of flatlands, prairies, big sky. I ask questions, look for evidence. There are no maps at congregation school. Wish I paid attention in Geography. There are no license plates, no tourist attractions, no nothing. I think this is Indiana. Folks are born into this crap-hole. Nobody comes here. Only my mother—once, sixteen years ago. And now me. I plan on leaving, just like her, real soon. Daylight they'd shoot me down like a scarecrow, straw-legged, flat on my back. Moon-guided nighttime, what scares them most, that's what I need. I have been here eleven nights. I think.

Supper is the second worst time of day. Father sits at the head, big tin plate in front. Large man-hands grasp the fork, the knife. He tucks the thick cloth in at his neck. He sits tall. Unforgiving. He commands silence, says grace, finally. When he finishes naming our earthly evils, the food is cold. Stepmother hops about like a sparrow, bringing seconds, adding the jellied side dish she forgot, a piece of pie. Her eyes bulge more, anticipate his whims. Provoke disdain.

Kyra chews. Kyra chews and eventually she swallows. Because she will need her strength to escape. She watches him and in her mind she brings him down a hundred dying ways. He chomps, teeth clacking, mouth open, mashed food churning vivid like clothes spinning at the laundromat. Father breathes loud, in and out his nose. Warmed air flutters the edge of her napkin; that's how close he is. That's how strong he is. Tufts of hair sprout from his nostrils, ears, the backs of his hands, the various ends of his shirt. She daydreams a morning without him.

My name is Kyra. I am brittle. Beneath my robot shell live Fury, Rage, and Vengeance. Ours will rise with the Moon tonight. With the Moon and with the tool I hid, stolen from the barn. Screwdriver. I have been here too many nights.

Kyra waits long into the dark. Hears a dog bark, bark, howl. Black as pitch—that's what they call this kind of dark. No windows, no night-lights, only the inner flame of putting a desperate plan to action. She folds down the bedclothes. She dresses slowly, stealthily. She carries her shoes. She stands on her side of the door, listening. There! Father snores from the other side of the cabin. She fits the metal screwdriver end, the flat edge, into the door crack, moves it gently, feels resistance. She sends her mind-power to the bolt, coaxes it to one side, tries to move it millimeter by millimeter to the right. To slide the bolt over. She stands until blood leaves her limbs, until her fingers hurt to hold it, and all her fiddling has left her nowhere. Sweat beads on her forehead. Kyra wants to cry. She leans against the door and feels a sharp jab on her spine. The hinge. She sniffs. She starts to work on those three pins, going by touch and hope and the powers churning within.

My name is Kyra. I am biding my time. Last night I loosened the pins in the door hinges. Tonight I wait and wait and pull them out. Then I pull the door. I lift the heavy wood and, with the leverage, I pull the bolt smoothly out of its casing. I set the door down—shit, it made a noise—I lean it on the bedroom wall. It scrapes a bit. I squeeze past. I move stealthy, magic, through the main sitting room in the dead dark and aim for the front door. Shuffle one step, hand held out in front, blinking like mad because there's no light, there's no window.

But there is something. It is tall and it grabs her arm. It is bearded, bad-breathed hissing. It's a clamping torture grip, a pulling, twisting, hurting and she says No. NO! Kyra struggles to the front door, is thrown against it. His hand tightens on her throat. Father commands her to stay, to fulfill his evil prophecy, to spawn his own. "To undo the hex, the curse, of that Heretic Woman."

I choke, I retch and shudder. I cannot breathe with those man-hands wrapped so tight. My strength ebbs. I remember the screwdriver, useful little tool, and raise it high. I plunge and thrust, I slide it deep between his ribs. I pound rhythmically, make him gasp and gurgle and whimper and wish it were not so. They are terrible, these sounds and smells of death row. The collapse and thrump of the heavy weight. I rub my neck, suck back air to those near-forgotten lungs. I reach for the handle and pull, pull the door wide open.

The pale hand appears in a flash, in a smash, and the wood is slammed shut again. Worse, Kyra's nightdress is stuck in there. Stepmother screams and claws, throttles her, snaps back Kyra's head. Batters her. "You filthy, sinful Jezebel!" She shrieks, bares her teeth, and with surprising force, tears at Kyra's skin. Kyra ducks, covers her face, crouches half on top of His body, while Stepmother kicks, hits. Then Kyra feels it and pulls for it and waits until Stepmother hesitates, Stepmother catches her breath. Still caught in the door, Kyra pushes upwards, as high as she can. She raises the tool.

I strike her in the bulgy eye. Again, again, and to the temple, to a crumpling, falling pile. And when I finally pull that latch and haul open the door and free my tattered night-skirt, I see that our screaming has wakened the entire village. Bathed in blood and moonlight, I dare any now to touch my fevered skin, dare them to prevent me, to hold me back, the Dark-Haired Devil Incarnate, truest daughter of my heretic mother. I call to the ghosty girls, but mostly to Alice, to come and fly with me, away. None but she will follow.

We run hard and fast, through the flattened miles of eternity, due north by the light of the moon. I know this as surely as I know my name is Kyra.

X X X X X

Kristyn Dunnion was born in Kingsville, Ontario, Home of The Goose. Her first book, Missing Matthew, *was published by Red Deer Press in 2003. Her second, also with Red Deer, is a punkrawk YA novel titled* Mosh Pit *(2004). She likes big boots, shaved heads, and loud music.*

BLOOD IS BLOOD

Anne Wessels

O ur family has a distinct absence of males. That's what my mother said before. I can only imagine what she'll say now.

x x x x x

The story begins with a phone call.

I pick up the receiver. "Hello?"

"Gretchen?" It's our downstairs neighbor, Pearl. "Get your mother. Where have you been? I've been trying to get a hold of you two."

"We were—"

"They've been calling me all afternoon. God, it's terrible. Something's happened. In Mexico."

x x x x x

The story continues in the air over Guadalajara.

As we begin our descent, I can see ridges of green mountains thousands of meters below. It looks like the ground has been crumpled together like an accordion. I turn to point this out to my mother but when I look over at her, I decide to wait for a better time. She stares straight ahead. Into the back of the seat ahead of her. This blank look is new, but shutting me out has been going on as long as I can remember.

So here we are with our seat belts on, descending into a city I've barely heard of, to visit a grandfather I've barely met. I begged to stay home and have the place to myself. But that didn't happen. Not after last time when the Ouija party went out of control and Pearl called the police. "Devil worshipers," she called us.

The plane shudders. When you start to really think about it— the true speed of this, I mean—you can start to doubt things. Like engineering and the strength of metal. We're just a thimble barreling toward the earth. Perhaps that's how the ground below became so crumpled. At one time it was flat, but the planes began to fall from the sky at tremendous speeds, denting the surface. I close my eyes and see metal piercing the earth followed by fiery explosions, sprays of blood, and then absolute and permanent silence.

X X X X X

The story continues on the ground at the Guadalajara airport.

My mother guides me to the exit and whispers to me, "Yellow taxis. Look for yellow taxis."

I look out and the sidewalk is lined with nothing but yellow taxis.

"At least something's going right," she says. "The others will say they're taxis and then you'll have your neck slit at the side of the road. Never to be found. A statistic."

"Mum," I say, and get into the back seat of the first yellow taxi and reach to find the seat belt.

"Is your belt on?" she asks.

"I'm trying but there's only half."

"That's it. Get out. We'll try the next one. *Gracias*," she says to the driver.

"Mum, it's fine. I'll be fine." I can feel my temper stirring. I hate it when she steamrolls me.

"No, we're out of here. One accident is enough."

We shuffle into the next taxi after she's tried all the seat belts.

"Hotel Lafayette, *por favor*," she reads from a scrap of paper to the driver with greasy hair. The back of his neck looks a lot like the accordion mountains we saw from the plane. I wonder how he cleans his valleys, or if they're filled with a lifetime of dirt and sweat, bread crumbs and hair oil.

x x x x x

The hotel is mouse-colored. Bleached to almost beige by the sun filtering through gauzy, useless curtains. Is there a worse color than beige? I would have preferred black. Are there any tropical resorts with black décor? At least this place isn't nearly as seedy as some of the motels Mum and I have stayed in, between apartments.

We enter the elevator with our luggage and room keys just as a beefy man with sweat stains under his arms squeezes between the closing doors.

"Don't get any hotter than this in Houston," he says. I can see that he's trying to open a conversation, but Mum shoots me a look that says, Button it up.

"Y'all from where?" he asks.

"Canada," I say.

"Here for a vacation in Meheeco?"

"Yes," I say.

"Our floor," Mum says.

We're only at the fourth floor, and I know from the room key that ours is the fifth.

"See y'all later," he says as the doors close between us.

Out in the hallway I say, "This is only the fourth, Mum."

"I know. Can't be too careful. Now, I wonder what staircase is in Spanish."

✗ ✗ ✗ ✗ ✗

The rain is so heavy that it films up the windshield of the taxi, and the city becomes an undulating blur of colors. We wind through streets jerked back and forth by accelerations and sudden braking. Does this driver even have a license? He wouldn't have a hope of passing in Toronto. My mother brakes on her side of the front seat.

The car comes to a stop and Mum reaches inside her denim shirt to find the money purse tied around her neck. She hands the driver the fare. As we get out, we see mist rising from the street. The short rain must have hit red-hot pavement.

Hanging beside the massive painted door in front of us is a brass plaque that says Hospital de la Paz. This could be a private home the way it comes right up to the sidewalk, the broken glass embedded in the stucco at the top of the wall.

We open the door and step across the threshold into a darkened foyer. An elderly nun looks up from her bench.

"Charles Easton, *por favor*," my mother says.

"*Un momento,*" says the nun with a hushed tone that warns us that this is a tight operation with quiet strictly enforced. She returns to the column of figures she seems to be adding on the clipboard on her lap.

We wait, not sure what to do next. Several long minutes pass before an energetic but equally fierce nun comes toward us.

"Charles Easton, *por favor,*" says my mother in a whisper. The nuns exchange glances and the younger one ushers us to a dreary waiting room. People are seated on wooden chairs that are bolted to the floor. Paint has chipped off the veal-colored walls. The nun gestures for me to sit and holds open a hospital gown for Mum.

My mother doesn't normally take direction well, but she puts her hands through the armholes without comment or resistance. Then they move through a door that closes behind them with a click that echoes through the silence of the waiting room.

As I wait, I try to read the signs. *Urgencias. Ortopedia y Traumatologia.* A brochure lies on the table from the Cruz Roja Mexicana. On the opposite wall there is a picture of a heart wound around and around with barbed wire. The heart bleeds where the barbs puncture it. It drips. I think it must have something to do with Jesus and his terrible suffering. I want to look away but this picture doesn't seem to let me go, like it's there to tell me something about my future. Something about why we've come and what's in store.

I pick at my cuticle until I feel the slight sting of blood. Something to break the spell of the painting. I force my eyes away from the bleeding heart to look down at my finger, but I sense that someone is watching me. I turn my head to find a woman who looks straight at me.

I lower my eyes.

She gets up and starts to come toward me but stops herself when she sees my mother come through the door with the nun. Mum is out of the gown now and she's very white. She keeps swallowing and sits down; her breathing is out of sync.

"What happened?" I ask.

"It's just much worse than we thought."

"What do you mean?"

"He's in intensive care. He's so sedated, he doesn't even know I'm here."

"Did you speak to a doctor?" I ask.

"Yes. It's touch and go."

"Do you think he's suffering?"

"Incredibly," she says.

"Like Jesus?" I ask.

"What?"

"Nothing," I say. I can feel that woman looking at me again. Or perhaps she's never stopped. She's smiling right at me. Her eyes are dog-like. Full of fake, overdone sympathy like she knows Jesus's pain. Like she knows what it's like to have a heart wound around with barbed wire.

There's something familiar about her. American—I can tell by her Docksider shoes. But something else. She's a feeder. You meet them sometimes. The biggest feeder I know is the social worker at school. Feeders feed on the pain of others. They pretend to feel, but they can't. Everyone knows they can't. Everyone but them, that is.

"Can we go back to the hotel?" I lean in to Mum and ask.

"Sure. Just give me a minute."

I miss Mum's military mode. It's just fallen away. You always think that you want to see the soft inside of your parent and then, when it happens, you just want them to close right back up again.

X X X X X

I can't eat any more of the *huevos rancheros*. They're watery and a little pool has collected on my plate, leaving my toast saturated and soggy. The fruit looks beautiful. Mango. Papaya. Pineapple.

"Nothing uncooked. We have to keep our strength," she says as she sips her coffee. The night's sleep has done her good.

"Do you think the doctor knows what he's doing?" I ask.

"He's our only hope."

"So, you do have hope?"

"Some. Finish up. We've got to meet him at ten so he can tell us what has happened in the night."

"He stays through the night?" I ask.

"I guess. Let's go."

"You always rush me," I say.

"Move it. I've got to go up and brush my teeth."

"Me too," I say. It does feel better now that she's back in charge.

X X X X X

At the elevator, the doors open and the Texan gets out.

"Morning, ladies," he says.

"Morning," we both say.

"What are the sisters up to today?" he asks.

"We're not sisters. She's my mother," I say.

"Could've fooled me," he says. He adjusts the toothpick in his mouth with one hand and holds the door to the elevator open for us with the other. "You got me curious: what brings you to this fine city, anyway?"

"We're visiting my grandfather in the hospital."

"Nothin' serious, I hope," he says.

"We're speaking to the doctor today. We'll know more this morning," my mother says in her sergeant major voice. I start to understand why men haven't exactly flocked to our family.

He lets the door go once we're inside, and he's finished with the conversation.

"Y'all have a good day," he says, and I think he really means it.

X X X X X

Once we get into our room, Mum runs to the bathroom and shuts the door behind her.

I check my eyeliner in the mirror. And tuck my new Dead Can Dance T-shirt into my belt. When I see my blonde roots, I wish there'd been time for a black dye-job before coming down here.

"Mum, are you almost ready?" I call.

But she doesn't answer. I go to the door to listen, but all I can hear is her breathing.

I go in and find her hunched over, sitting on the toilet.

"I don't feel so good, Gretch."

"Stomach?" I ask.

"Crampy and the runs," she says.

I take a washcloth and douse it in water from our drinking bottle and take it over to her. I can see beads of sweat on her forehead and on either side of her nose. She's as white as when she came out of intensive care yesterday.

She breathes as if she can't quite get enough air into her lungs.

"Should I call for help?" I ask.

"No," she says, and she gets down on the tile floor and pulls her legs up into the fetal position.

"What about the doctor?" I ask.

"Get the money out of my wallet and go," she says.

"I'll just wait for you." I feel like I'm starting to sweat. For a moment I hope I come down with this thing so I can avoid going by myself.

"Gretchen, you've got to go. He needs one of us."

"He barely knows me."

"You're blood. Hospital de La Paz. Avenida Augustin Yanez. Now go."

"You'll feel better soon, and we'll go together."

"Get going," she says.

"I don't think I should leave you."

"Just go," she insists.

X X X X X

There's a stump of a nun at the front door of the hospital who looks up at me, and then back to her reading. She registers no emotion on her face, as if she's worn out by all these years of pain and suffering and disease.

In the waiting room I look straight at the painting of the bleeding heart. I swear I can see it contract as if it's trying to pump like a real heart. I've never believed in signs before, but I do now. Yesterday and today. Signs. Loud and clear. I know for sure that my grandfather hasn't died in the night. I just know.

"*Senora* Luks?" asks a man in a white lab coat as he approaches me.

"No, I'm her daughter, Gretchen." I reach out my hand to shake his. "She's sick this morning, so I've come, and whatever you tell me, I'll go back to the hotel and tell her."

"Fine. To start, the situation is very serious. His lungs seem to have suffered some trauma from the accident. Fluid is not draining and this is the real danger."

"Do you think he'll make it?" I ask.

"I would say that his chances are less than fifty percent, but I've seen people who are worse survive." He pauses. "I think you should go in."

"Are you sure?"

"Yes, it might strengthen him."

"He probably won't even recognize me."

"You're his granddaughter. Blood is blood," he says as he hands the gown to me.

I lift my head, breathe in, and put one foot in front of the other. I can feel the beat of my heart. He holds the door for me to pass through. It clicks shut behind us. He leads me down a corridor with bare light bulbs hanging from the ceiling. We pass one door after another until we reach number fifteen. He opens it and ushers me through.

Machines hiss. Monitors beep as beads of light trip across their screens. The air has been breathed too many times. Hushed voices whisper.

My grandfather lies immobile, but propped upright in his hospital bed. Tubes leave his nose and his open mouth. They also come out from under his blanket and empty into a closed canister under his bed.

The doctor nudges me forward so that I can be seen. As I get closer, I see cuts on my grandfather's forehead that are stitched closed. My stomach seizes. His swollen lips are badly chapped. His hair stands on end, as if he is in a permanent state of terror, and what he sees behind his closed eyes is nothing but shattering glass, crumpling metal, and blood.

Dark yellow circles lie under his eyes. I realize that to let him know I'm here, I'll have to speak. Just as I am about to, I hear shrieking from another bed. A nun scuttles over and within seconds quiet resumes.

"Grandpa?" I say.

He doesn't respond. His eyes stay shut. All that moves is his chest going up and down too quickly to be restful.

"Grandpa, it's Gretchen, and Mum's here too, but she's sick today."

I don't know what to say next. I feel like I need to sit down. But there aren't any chairs close by. "I hope you feel better. You will. You have to think you will, and you will," I say.

Listen to me. Here I am like all the feeders I've ever known who say things just to make people feel better. They can't bear to tell the real truth. Since when do I believe in the power of positive thinking?

I look to the doctor for help, but he's moved to the desk at the central nurses' station where he checks some notes.

He looks up and I motion toward the door, asking for permission to leave. He lifts his finger to delay me, puts down his clipboard and comes over.

"Done?" he asks as if he's a bit surprised.

"Yes. I'll come back later." Can he tell that I'm losing to the fear that has engulfed every cell of my being?

He opens the door of the unit. I'm weak, I know, but I just have to get out of here.

"'Bye, Grandpa," I say. "I'll be back soon. Mum's here and we'll be back. I promise."

x x x x x

By the time I've stripped off my gown and yanked open the door to the waiting room, I can feel pins and needles in my hands. I sit down because if I don't, I'll topple over. I think of some of my friends at school, especially the ones with the black clothes and the spiky jewelry. We say we worship death, but I don't think we have any idea. No one in their right mind would worship this.

The feeder woman is holding out to me a cross she's wearing around her neck. She tilts her head at me, like she wants my soul for Jesus if I would just give in. She knows the weakness in my heart and my raging fear. She knows all about me, and to protect what little soul I have, I look away like this happens every day and I can handle everything without her and definitely without Jesus. Her idea of Jesus, at least.

"Is there someplace to get a drink?" I ask the doctor.

"There's a *cantina* through the courtyard. If you get to the chapel, you've gone too far." He points to get me started in the right direction.

"Would you like one?" I ask him.

"Thank you, no. I have to get to the other hospital."

"When will you be back? So I can tell my Mum. She might be better by then."

"I can meet you at ten o'clock tonight."

"It might be hard to come back tonight," I say.

"But your promise," the doctor says.

"What?" I ask.

"You told him that you would come back. There might not be another chance."

"You're right," I say. Every minute that I'm here I feel flimsier and flimsier.

I squint to make my way across the open-air courtyard, fighting the blinding sun. All around me are flowers in full bloom, but they seem to be bleached pale.

I buy my Coca-Cola and take it to the edge of one of the flower beds and sit. I down it. I don't even pause to breathe until it's done. It's not that it tastes so good; just familiar. I take a closer look at the flowers. They're all wound around one another, and white maggots wriggle on the earth where someone has thrown some old tortillas.

This is too much. I just don't have what it takes. Mum had better get up and running. Now.

✗ ✗ ✗ ✗ ✗

The smell hits me the moment I come back into the hotel room. The curtains are drawn but there's enough light to see that she has moved back to the bed and is sleeping. She needs Coca- Cola. I'll have it ready for her when she wakes up.

I go back down to the lobby to buy some. On the way back up, the Texan enters the elevator. "How's your-all's grandfather today?"

"He's no better. Worse, I'd say."

"Sorry to hear that. Tequila's a great healer, you know," he says.

I look at him as if that's the stupidest thing I've ever heard.

"Not for him. For you. Calm your nerves. Give you strength," he says.

"Sorry." I feel trapped, like he's only saying half of what he means. I look to see if there's an emergency button, but before I do anything I realize we've come to my floor.

"See you later, alligator," he says and winks at me. I feel like I need to take a long shower.

His aftershave's clogged my pores.

✗ ✗ ✗ ✗ ✗

"Mum, you should drink something," I say.

"Not now."

"No, you have to drink to make up for what you've lost."

"It'll just come back up," she says.

"Come on, try."

"Get out of my face," she says.

All I want is to take one of those yellow cabs back to the airport and fly home and leave them both to die. In the same city, but all alone. You treat people this way, you die alone. You don't have to be good to people at the end of their lives just because they're blood, do you?

A thin strip of light from the gap in the curtains hits a piece of modern art hanging on the wall. Here in the semi-darkness with the stench of vomit, the red paint that looks like smeared blood peels off the painting as if it just can't lie flat a moment longer. As if the blood-red paint has to move out into another dimension, out into the room for some sinister purpose I can't even begin to imagine.

I start to imagine my own skin peeling away from the muscle. My flesh opening up until I, too, will lose my life in Guadalajara with nuns who do nothing but add and subtract, and Christians who just stand by and smile, and mothers who can't even get out of bed.

I take the bottle of Coke and hold up my mother's head. "You have to drink whether you like it or not," I say. "We've got to go."

"It tastes so good," she says as she takes her first tentative sips.

"Now get up," I say.

I gather my knapsack and head to the door.

"Gretchen?" she calls.

"What?"

"Get the garbage can. Fast." I put it beside her bed just in time and she vomits into it. One thing's clear: I'm still on my own. She won't be heading anywhere today but the bathroom.

"Gretchen," she calls.

"What?" I ask.

"Wait."

"I've got to go."

"Gretchen, thanks," she says as she wipes her forehead and settles back onto her pillows.

I don't say anything. I just dump the contents of the garbage can into the toilet and flush.

x x x x x

Driving back to the hospital in the taxi, I see a store-front window full of caskets. They're alive with light. The light after the daily downpour. Red satin drapery shimmers. Gold lettering glitters above the doorway. I feel a pull to the future, a pull to destruction. A pull I don't have the strength to resist.

x x x x x

The doctor is in the waiting room in his white lab coat. He's ashen and the circles under his eyes are darker and more sunken. When he sees me, he inhales, squares his shoulders, and walks toward me.

He takes my elbow and guides me to a chair.

"Things are very bad—growing infection in his body, and he is only able to use a small amount of oxygen from each breath. If we can't find some way to reverse this, your grandfather will die."

He's preparing me, just the way Jesus and his bared heart and the painting in the hotel room and the caskets have prepared me.

"Go, speak to him. Be with him," he says to me.

I gown up, walk the hallway to door fifteen and enter. On first glance, it doesn't look worse to me.

"Grandpa," I start.

His eyes are still closed. Even though I search his being for some sign, I really have no hope for a response. But could he hear me? I don't know that he can't.

"Grandpa, you have to know that Mum loves you," I start. "It's not easy for her. But she got us here. Bought plane tickets. We never travel anywhere. Moving every year has kept us busy.

"Mum's at the hotel. She's really sick. She wants to see you but she just can't. You know she's tried to be a good mother. In her own way.

"She's all alone except for me. After Dad left she lost all her energy. Sometimes I'd worry that she'd hurt herself. I'd imagine coming home and there she'd be, hanging from something, dead. So I stopped going to school. I needed to take care of her, make sure she ate and everything. Well, then the social worker got involved, and as much as I didn't want her around, she tried to listen to me and get Mum some help.

"I'm behind at school, but I'll get there sooner or later. So if you have to die—and I hope that you don't—but if you have to, you can leave and know that we're okay now. We'll be okay."

"Excuse me," the doctor says. His voice is controlled but the fierceness of his eyes betrays his fear. "We have a procedure we would like to try. Could we ask you to kindly wait in the waiting room?"

After I leave I can hear the door lock behind me.

I hover in the hallway. I hear a rush of people behind the ICU door. I hear the doctor call out orders in Spanish, and there's such a sense of urgency that it seems to seep through the walls. I hear a body flop. The sound of flesh hitting a hard surface. Shouts. I want to break back in and ask them to stop. Just to let him be, let him go in peace. But I can't move. I can't speak.

After a stretch of time—maybe minutes, maybe seconds—the doctor comes into the hall. He's surprised to see me. He knows what I've overheard. I search his face for a sign that this last-ditch measure has been a success.

"Your grandfather has passed away," the doctor says.

He takes my elbow and leads me back into the unit to the side of my grandfather's bed. They've removed the tubes. And he's naked, but for cotton they have wrapped around his middle. Like swaddling clothes.

The world is still. Holy night, silent night. One moment suspended. That instant when you have breathed in, just before you breathe out. It's the moment after hope. When she's just walked away, and you can't get there fast enough to tug at her skirts to pull her back.

He's just a body. Dead. And this thing called life—it just goes. Just leaves.

"Thank you for being my grandfather," I say.

There are no more words. This is the end of words. The end of possibility.

✗ ✗ ✗ ✗ ✗

The doctor leads me back to the waiting room, and I start to shake. He sits me down. The Christian woman comes over and speaks. "Go ahead and cry."

I just lift my hand to stop her, but she closes in. She still wants me for Jesus. She wants my heart all wound around with barbed wire. But my heart is strangely calm. It isn't bleeding, ripped away. It's filled with love. With loss.

"Fuck off," I tell her. "Doctor, can you walk with me to the chapel?"

He leads me past the flowers and the maggots, past the *cantina* that's closed now.

"I'm okay," I say, and he lets me walk down the aisle into the back pew by myself. I hold my hands together in my lap and think of my mum and all the words she didn't say. And I think of all the love in the world, and the moment when life leaves the body. And here I am, one creature on this vast earth, here with my body intact, and the breath going in and going out.

After a time, the nuns rustle in, silent but for their footsteps on the tiles and their skirts brushing past each other. They begin their morning hymns, and the voices wind in and around one another as they travel up the stone walls and up over the wooden beams, and out into the air of the world. Cradling my heart, singing for the sick and the dying and the dead. These leaden faces with music so deep inside them and on their breath. A gift to the morning. Giving thanks for the world and all the sadness and imperfection in it. Giving thanks, giving thanks.

✗ ✗ ✗ ✗ ✗

The story doesn't end here. There are death certificates and instructions to the morgue and all night at the funeral home and casket choices and funerals and the crematorium and waiting for ashes. But that's later. Now we're right where the story started. How do I tell my mother that the last of the men is gone? Her estranged father—but father all the same—has died.

x x x x x

I sit on the edge of her bed.

"I was with him and told him that you love him and that we're okay. Now."

"Gretchen, you're a good soul."

"Blood is blood, Mum."

x x x x x

And this is where the story ends. My mother reaches for my hand and gently strokes it as we stare out into the darkened hotel room together.

X X X X X

Anne Wessels's short story, "Could You Be Attracted to Me?" won first prize in the Writing for Children Awards in the 2004 Writers' Federation New Brunswick annual Literary Competition. Her short story, "The World is Too Vast to Know Everything About Everything," was commissioned by the Canada Council and the CBC, and was broadcast on CBC Radio's Festival of Fiction in October, 2001. Born in Toronto, Anne now teaches drama for the Peel District School Board. She has acted professionally in theaters in Canada and the United States, and is a graduate of the National Theater School of Canada, the University of Toronto, and Queen's University.

GRAVEYARD STUDIES

Sylvo Frank

"Hey, Tony—check this out." Nick is standing before the entrance of the McDonnell family vault, his hand on the doorknob. Hinges creak as he opens the massive metal door.

"How'd you do that?"

"Duh. I used the doorknob."

"It wasn't locked?"

"Apparently not." Nick smiles, then steps inside. "C'mon!"

I glance around. As far as I can tell, we're alone in this neck of the graveyard. I follow Nick in.

"Velcome to my vault!" Nick's no more Transylvanian than I am, but he does a good impression.

"We probably shouldn't be in here."

"Hey, the door was open, so why not? It's not like we're grave robbers or anything. Besides, we've got the perfect excuse: graveyard studies."

Graveyard studies. We say it together and we both laugh.

Brathwaite gave all his grade nines the assignment on Remembrance Day: learn about history by collecting info from a local graveyard and analyzing it, searching for clues about the past.

Part 1: Record the names of 50 deceased, along with their dates of birth and death, and anything else inscribed on their headstones. (Beloved Wife of Harold Bartholomew. Nearer My God to Thee.)

We've already done this.

Part 2: Record the following about each grave's marker: upright stone or plaque? Is there anything unusual about the marker? (I.e., carved angels on top?) If so, draw an image of it.

I let Nick do the drawing. He's way better at it. I almost failed art.

What material are the markers made of? Duh, stone, of course. But what kind of stone? Mostly granite, it turns out. Some marble too, though.

Part 3: Why was this site chosen for the graveyard? How the hell should I know?

Part 4: Are there any family vaults in the graveyard? Eight, at least. *If so, briefly describe one.* Okay, this one.

Exterior: pretentious fake-Greek columns. Makes the place look like a teeny-tiny bank.

Interior: A chamber about one and a half coffins wide, two deep and six stacked coffins high. Stone slabs line the side walls, each slab with its own brass handles and plaque bearing the name of someone dead—whoever's corpse is on the other side, I suppose.

"Enough roses for you?" Nick pokes his nose into a huge bouquet of white ones sitting on a pedestal at the rear of the vault. "Hmm, not much scent."

I sit down on a bench next to the flowers; it's cold to the touch, smooth. White marble, like everything else in here. No surprise, really, considering how rich the McDonnells are. The only splash of color in the place comes from the stained glass window above the roses: God the Father, all radiant at the top of the window, shines his light onto the flock of saints below him and onto the humans below them.

Part 4B: What role does this family play in the community? They lord it over the rest of us.

"Hey Tony, this guy just died last week!" That explains the fresh flowers, and the open door. Someone must have just visited and then forgotten to lock it. I get up, walk over to the plaque Nick's looking at. Malcolm McDonnell. The name jogs my memory.

"He made the news on Friday," I say. "Front page of all the papers."

"And now the rich bastard's RIP-ing. So sad, too bad."

"Jeez, Nick, have some respect for the dead."

"Yes, Dad." We both burst out laughing.

A ray of pink light beams in through the open door, coloring the wall beside us. For a second, I imagine being trapped in here for the night, just me and the corpses. I shiver.

"It's getting late," I say. "We should get out of here before they lock the gates."

"My child, do not be afraid of the dark." There's that Transylvanian accent again.

"I'm not. I just don't want to have to climb over the gate or the wall."

"My child, do not be afraid of a little exercise."

"You wouldn't want to tear your jeans trying to get out of here, would you?"

"My child, do not worry. I will turn into a bat and fly over the barriers easily, easily."

I roll my eyes, then check my watch. Almost 5:30. Closing time. We step out of the vault and close the door behind us, then head back toward the gate. We've got a ways to go.

The sky's turning darker overhead; the first stars make their appearance.

Part 5: Statistical analysis: What patterns can you discern in the collected information? (Hint: Look for clusters of deaths due to wars, epidemics, etc.)

Sylvo Frank

Part 5B: Do the ethnicities of the dead and the dates of their births and deaths correspond to known waves of immigration to the area? Support your conclusions.

"So, Nicholas Bryce, do the ethnicities of the dead and the dates of their births and deaths correspond to known waves of immigration to the area?"

Nick stops, leans against a high tombstone and rubs his chin. "Well, clearly *my* people got here long before *your* people made it over in their pasta-laden boats."

"Hey, watcha whadda you say abouta my people."

"Admit it: they used salamis for oars. That's why they took so long to get here."

The clang of metal on metal cuts the air. "Damn," I say. "Now we're going to have to climb over the gate."

"Hey, isn't that Dora up ahead?"

"Where?"

"Shhh! Get down!" Nick drags me down behind a tombstone, then points to a spot near the top of the next hill. There she is, head hunkered down, hurrying toward the gate. She must have been working on Brathwaite's assignment too.

Nick whispers in my ear. "Let's sneak up on her and scare her."

"You think she saw us?"

"Nah. She's facing the other direction."

"I don't know, Nick. She's might think we're rapists or something."

"Oh, come on. We're not going to *really* scare her. Besides, how often do you get to sneak up on someone in a graveyard at night?"

I see his point. We dart from tombstone to tombstone like bats, or weasels, maybe, inching toward our prey. Tiny bubbles of guilt rise up within me, but I squelch them for the sake of the chase. Dora still hasn't clued in. Then a wind rises, and she stops dead in her tracks. She turns and looks directly toward us, but we're crouching behind a bush and I don't think she can see us, let alone recognize us. She bolts though, like a startled deer or something, so

I guess she must have figured out someone's there. Nick and I shift into high gear. We giggle as we lope after her, a pair of wolves in hot pursuit, all giddy and excited.

Boy, will she ever be pissed when she realizes it's just us. She's been so testy lately, but hey, she'll get over it. I mean, we've known her since kindergarten and she's always sort of liked us even though we've always played tricks on her. Besides, I think she's got the hots for me.

Dora zigzags, trying to lose us, but we stay on her tail. She circles around and instead of heading toward the gate, she runs deeper into the graveyard. Nick and I start panting. We really shouldn't skip gym so often—my lungs are shocked. We slow down, then come to a stop. We're back at the McDonnell vault. I clutch my side, try to catch my breath. Nick calls out, "Dora, stop! It's just us! Nick and Tony!" But she keeps on running, even though I'm sure she's heard Nick and recognizes his voice. "Hey, stop! We were just joking!" But she's running even faster now, so we keep on chasing her. We could just let her go, but I want to make sure she's okay, and that she's not too angry at us. I guess I sort of want to apologize.

Finally she stops. I'm relieved, but then she turns, glares at us, and hollers. "Get lost! Go away!"

Ooh, she's angry.

"Dora, look," says Nick, "we were just—"

"Run!" She screams it at us. "Run! Get away from me! Go home!" Then she takes off, still deeper into the graveyard.

"Dora, we're sorry," I shout. "Stop!"

Moonlight floods the hillside, painting Dora a ghoulish bluish-white. She falls to the ground. She doesn't get up. "Dora!" We run to her, kneel beside her still body. She starts convulsing.

"Shit!" says Nick. "Is she epileptic? Is she having a seizure?"

"I don't know. Fuck! What do you do for a seizure?"

"How should I know? Hold her down? Make sure she doesn't hurt herself?"

Dora starts moaning like someone possessed. Nick moves her head away from a nearby tombstone, then holds her down. "Go get help," he says.

I head for the gate as fast as I can until I hear Nick calling. "Tony!" Something in his voice makes me stop, turn around. He's one hill back and running. For a second I wonder why he's left Dora, but then Nick sees me and shouts, "Run!" Before I can move, though, I hear growls coming from where Dora fell, and then I see . . . what? A dog, is it? A wolf? *A wolf?* In the city? It's huge. If it's a dog, it's a monster dog, some sort of über-dog. I stand transfixed and stare at the beast—then I realize it's chasing Nick. I'm about to call out, but the hound catches up to him, pounces on his back and knocks him over, then rips open his throat.

I can't believe what I'm seeing. I want to scream, but no sound comes out of my mouth. The beast howls, then turns and looks right at me, its blood-smeared teeth gleaming in the moonlight.

I run. Fear drives me. The beast pursues.

It's gaining on me. I can't make it to the gate before it gets me, but maybe I can reach the vault. My muscles burn, my heart pounds; I will myself to the open door and through it, then slam it shut. I can't lock the deadbolt without a key, so I jiggle the doorknob and tug on it, just to make sure at least the latch is securely in its hole in the doorpost. It is. I lean back against the door, panting, then feel it shudder in its frame as the beast slams into it again and again, howling all the while.

I feel like one of the three fucking little pigs. Thank God I've got a house of stone and canines don't have opposable thumbs.

Outside, the beast paces, growling, howling. Then silence. I wonder what it's doing, but I'm not opening the door to find out. Instead, I peek out one of the door's tiny, square windows, only to see a big, yellow eye up against the glass, watching me. I jump back and the beast howls. I see its teeth, its tongue; then it's gone from view.

I retreat to the rear of the vault, sit on the bench and cover my face with clammy hands. I force myself to take a deep breath, then another. I can't hear the beast. I lift my head, open my eyes. On the floor before me, I see God, or at least an image of him cast there by moonlight pouring through the stained glass. Thankfully, I also see the shadow of metal bars crisscrossing the window, protecting both the dead and me. I stand up, turn to the window, and bathe in the colored light for a moment, but then the beast's shadow blocks it. My chest tightens, then I scream as a paw smashes through the glass, sending shards of splintered saints hurtling though the air.

To my horror, the paw reaches my face and scratches it—a shallow cut, but it burns like acid. The beast's howling now. I can see it through the broken window, see its liquid lips glistening, its eyes spinning in the moonlight, and I'm feeling dizzy. I can hear the beast dashing and yipping and howling all around the vault, a mad rage of a dance. The raw moonlight tingles on my skin. My body's shaking now and it's too much. Can't stand my clothes, can't bear them on my skin, can't bear anything, can't stand the sight of me, the smell of me, can't stand the walls, the stone. I've got to get out of here, but I can't, I can't. I can't even stand up, I'm shaking too badly. I fall over, I scream, I moan.

God, I can smell her outside and I want her, want her, want her and she wants me, she's panting for me. I can hear her, I know her scent and I can't bear it, I've got to get out of here. I bash against the wall and I howl, I fumble with the doorknob but my fingers don't work. I'm trapped, trapped. I could scream just scream just scream. Could scream—"*Waooooo! Waoooo! Waoooo! Waoooo! Waoooo!*"

X X X X X

Sirens wake me up—that and the smell of pickled corpse, and blood, dried blood, and cum. My dick's throbbing. I reach down and stroke it. Yup, it's my own cum I'm smelling; I'm slathered in it. I run my sticky fingers up my belly, my chest, over my chin, my lips, to my nose. Strange, my cum smells different, skankier. It even tastes different. I like it.

God, I'm sore. I think about getting up, but my body refuses, so I just open my eyes and look around. What a mess. Roses scattered all over the floor and broken glass and clothes—my clothes, I think. Sunlight pours in through a broken stained glass window.

I recognize this place. It's a burial vault. I think I've been here before. Maybe with Nick. Maybe yesterday. Was I here yesterday?

I smell leather too. A hunk of sole lies near my head along with a couple of laces. Someone's been chewing on my shoe.

What the hell am I doing here? I seem to remember a cut on my cheek, but my cheek's as smooth as the marble I'm lying on, except for the hair. I need a shave, but that can wait. Hey, I'm not going anywhere just yet. I mean, all things considered, I feel pretty damn good, so why rush? Where have I got to go that's so important? *School?*

I hear voices outside. Three men, I can smell them: reek-of-testosterone. One had coffee and donuts for breakfast. Another had his wife; weird but I think I can smell her too. And the third—well, he had to settle for bacon and eggs.

I hope they go away, but no such luck. "Hello. This is the police. Is anybody in there?"

I think about the moon and smile.

"Hello. This is the police. Is there—"

Yeah, yeah.

Coffee-and-Donuts moves around to the back. The other two stay out front. "We're here to help you. Can you speak?"

The full moon is an incredible thing—

"Put your arms out where we can see them."

—alive.

"We're coming in."

And there they are, guns drawn. They check me for weapons, then ask questions. How am I? Who am I? What happened? I ignore them, but they don't take the hint. They babble to each other. Soon more arrive. It's a party now. They take photographs, videotape. My dick'll be famous.

Now medics. They babble too, but I don't care. Next thing I know, I'm on a stretcher. Out I go, into the morning sunlight.

When I get home, I'm going to have a steak. Rare, I think. Maybe two. Won't Mama be surprised.

X X X X X

Although a Winnipegger by birth, Sylvo Frank has lived most of his life in Toronto, where he has been a waiter, clown, musician, stilt walker, futon maker, leather craftsman, and is currently a child care worker. His story "The Fox and the Wolf" appears in the anthology At the Edge: A Book of Risky Stories *(Ragweed Press: 1998). It is excerpted from his self-published book,* A Fox's Tale.

REVENGE

Karleen Bradford

D arlene stared at Franny Dickson. What was that expression her boring, boring counselor had used yesterday? "If looks could kill." That was it.

"Darlene, if looks could kill, I think I'd be toast right now. Why can't you get it into your head that I'm trying to help you?"

Whine, whine. She had the whiniest voice on the planet. And the dumbest vocabulary. Right out of ancient history.

If looks could kill, freaky Franny would be so dead right now. Look at her. Flirting with Tod. Flirting! As if she didn't know the only reason he'd chosen her for his Chem partner was because she was such a droning brain. Pathetic.

Darlene had even offered to partner Tod herself. She flushed as she remembered his awkward refusal.

"Um . . . Thanks, Darlene, but I . . . uh . . . I already asked someone."

He hadn't, of course. She knew very well he hadn't asked freaky Franny until yesterday. She'd heard him. She was just as smart as freaky Franny, and she was better looking too. What was it with him, anyway?

She got up from the lab stool and stretched. Walked up to Mr. Henderson's desk. Could she help it if she accidentally jostled freaky Franny's arm?

Of course Franny had to scream and make a big deal of it. Disrupt the whole class while she scrubbed her hand.

"That was clumsy, Darlene," Mr. Henderson said.

Even Tod glared at her.

So what?

She rolled her eyes and dropped down onto her stool with an exaggerated sigh. Her two best friends were watching her, and covering up giggles. She'd impressed them, anyway. Not that *that* was hard to do. Morons.

"Did you see the burn on Freaky's hand?" Mel asked. "Tod said she should have a doctor look at it."

"Awesome," Sylvia agreed.

Darlene didn't bother to answer. She knew very well that Franny's hand wasn't burned. Mr. Henderson kept too careful a watch over the class for that. But if they wanted to make a big deal out of it, why not?

She didn't see why Tod had to make such a fuss over her, though.

Lunch in the cafeteria was the usual feeding time at the zoo. By now Darlene's mood had flamed from anger into full-fledged fury. Seeing Tod throw his arm around Franny's shoulder as they walked down the hall ahead of her caused her stomach to knot in actual pain. When he bent his head down to her, when she lifted her face up to his, their lips almost touching, the cramp grabbed her in such a vise that she stumbled and had to bend over to draw breath. She slammed her tray down on the table.

"Hey!" Sylvia cried, grabbing for her can of pop as it fell over and spilled.

Phys Ed was last period. Basketball for the girls in the gym. That was one period Darlene liked. There was something about the speed of the game—the power she felt when she had the ball in her control. The school was old, though, and the gym was just a big room way down in the basement. How great it would be to be able to play in a proper basketball court! She could really show them all then. What a hope. She shrugged, slipped her team's sash over her head and ran out onto the court. Franny ran out from the other side, stumbled and almost fell.

"Look at her," Darlene sneered out of the corner of her mouth to Mel. "That girl is so messed!"

Darlene's team won—they usually did—but Mel and Sylvia were the only ones who rushed to congratulate her on her playing. She'd scored three baskets: you'd think her teammates would be grateful. Not them. They acted as if she wasn't even there.

"You could have a lot more friends if you just tried, Darlene," the counselor had said. As if Darlene cared. As if it was any of that stupid woman's business, anyway. She stripped off her sash and tossed it in a heap on the floor with all the others.

"Franny," Ms. Rogers called, "would you put the sashes away in the sports locker, please?"

"Sure thing," Franny answered with a smile.

Sucky as ever, Darlene thought. Franny was red-faced and sweating. Limp, soaking-wet strands of hair were plastered down on her forehead, dripping into her eyes.

Too bad Tod can't see her now.

Ms. Rogers left and the other girls swarmed after her.

"Coming, Darlene?" Sylvia called. She and Mel were hanging back, waiting for her.

"In a minute," Darlene answered. "You guys go on ahead."

She watched Franny tossing the sashes into the locker.

Mel and Sandra left. Franny was leaning in, trying to straighten something out at the back. There was no one else in the gym now, no sound but her own heavy breathing and Franny's rummaging away.

How easy it would be. . . .

She grinned.

One push and Franny toppled over onto the pile of sashes and balls. Darlene slammed the locker door. She heard it click shut.

"Hey!" Franny's voice was muffled. "Who did that? Who closed the door?"

Darlene grinned even more widely. She knew there was no handle on the inside.

"Open the door!" There was a note of panic in Franny's voice.

Darlene turned away. She bent down to retie the lace on one shoe, straightened up, then left the gym.

See how you like that, Franny Driscoll. See how long it takes you to get out of there!

X X X X X

The next morning, when she pushed open her home room door, she was met with a buzz of excitement.

"Have you heard?" Mel gasped, her eyes wide. "Franny Driscoll's disappeared!"

"Her parents are frantic," Sylvia put in. "They've called the police."

Darlene's stomach gave a lurch. She couldn't still be in the locker. No way could she still be in the locker. If nobody else had found her first, the custodian would have—surely he checked things before going home at night. Didn't he?

The loudspeaker crackled into life.

"There's been an accident," the voice of their principal boomed out. It sounded shaky, totally unlike his usual good-natured chortle. "A terrible accident. . . ."

X X X X X

School was closed for the rest of the day. Grief counselors would be on hand the following day for any students who wanted to come in.

Darlene left with Mel and Sylvia, but they were curiously quiet. Instead of walking with her, they both made excuses.

"I'm in a hurry today," Mel said.

"Have to drop by my mom's store," Sylvia said.

Neither one of them would meet her eyes.

"What?" Darlene demanded.

They backed off.

"You don't think *I* shut her in there, do you?

"You were the last person . . ." Mel began, then gulped and swallowed whatever else she was about to say.

"It was an accident!" Darlene cried. "You heard what Mr. Pringle said. An accident!"

"They say her fingers were all bloody and her nails torn off from trying to claw her way out," Sylvia said.

"She was claustrophobic, her parents said," Mel added.

Darlene whirled away from them and ran to the corner of her street. Once around it, she looked back but the two girls had disappeared. A cold wind had come up and it was spitting rain. She hunched her chin down into her jacket and hugged herself to keep warm, but she couldn't stop shaking.

And then it was as if something shifted. As if something rearranged itself around her.

x x x x x

When she got home there was a note on the refrigerator door.

Working late tonight. Pizza in the fridge. Help yourself.

She couldn't eat. She stumbled up to her room and threw herself down on her bed.

It wasn't my fault! It was just a joke! How was I supposed to know that moron was claustrophobic? How was I supposed to know the custodian had gone home early? It wasn't my fault!

She lay there until the room darkened and the street lamp outside her window came on. She made no move to get up and draw the curtains. Rain slashed against the window and the wind howled.

She didn't think it would be possible, but she must have slept.

When she awoke the room was dark and quiet. Too dark. Too quiet. No sound of rain, no sound of wind. No sound of anything. No light. Had the street lamp burned out? It was so dark, she couldn't even see the outline of her window. She sat up. The air felt heavy. She swung her legs over the side of the bed. The floor was cold. Icy. She stood up and felt her way down to the end of the bed, then stretched out her hand to where the light switch should be on the wall.

Strange. It wasn't there. She felt along the wall. No switch. That wasn't right. She shuffled forward, reached the corner, then felt along the wall for the window. It was so dark! She couldn't see a thing.

Where was the window? The wall seemed to go on far longer than it should. And her desk? Her desk was underneath the window. She was walking carefully, taking care not to bump into it, but it wasn't there. No posters tacked up beside it. Nothing! A needle of fear stabbed through her.

The wall was smooth. Slippery. She kept her hand running along it. Whatever was happening here, she didn't dare lose contact with it.

She came to another corner.

I'm dreaming, she told herself. Wake up!

But the wall felt too real. Too solid.

She forced herself to move forward again. Her bookcase was along this wall. There was a pile of books on the floor beside it. Her backpack. She'd thrown her backpack down on the floor right here!

She stopped, reached down, felt around. Nothing.

This can't be happening, she repeated to herself. She kept saying it over and over.

The fear was a huge, raw lump in her throat now; she could hardly breathe around it.

Her outstretched hand found another corner.

Turn back! No, she couldn't turn back. She didn't even dare turn around!

This had to be the wall where the door was. Just let her feel the doorknob and she'd be out of here. Out in the hallway. Her mom must be home by now. There would be light there. She could get her bearings.

No door . . . bare wall . . . and a fourth corner.

Panic rose sour in her mouth. Her heart was pounding so hard it was shaking her whole body.

My bed. Just let me get back to my bed!

She almost ran forward in the dark.

It should be here. . . . It must be here!

It wasn't.

With a terrified sob, she struck at the wall, pounded it. Then she staggered back, off balance. And hit the opposite wall. It was right behind her. She whirled around, took a step forward, was brought up short by another wall.

Impossible!

She spun around again. The fourth wall was so close she couldn't move.

Nothing but walls on all sides of her. Enclosing her. Closing in on her. . . .

She screamed.

But no one heard.

X X X X X

Karleen Bradford was born in Toronto, and has published nineteen books of fiction and non-fiction for children and young adults. She has received several awards, including the 1993 Canadian Library Association Award for the Best Young Adult Novel of the Year and the Max and Greta Ebel Award for a Canadian author of children's books whose work best contributes to a greater understanding among people of different backgrounds, cultures and/or generations. Her work includes historical and contemporary novels and fantasy. She is a full-time writer now, but worked for many years as a group social worker in an after-school program for children and teens.

BOGEYMAN

Rob Morphy

The police are coming. Dana is playing in her room. She is two years old, Sarah's child, full of the same wide-eyed innocence. Her fresh scent draws me like a fly to an open wound. My teeth chatter, my nails rake the doorframe, I snort and drool like a beast. She looks around at me and laughs. It's a game to her.

I remember how from time to time Sarah would bring her hand up to tuck the hair behind her ear. She'd catch herself and scratch her bald head or straighten her cap. In the photos she showed me her hair was shoulder length, wavy, medium brown. I wish I could have run my fingers through it.

Dana's hair is like her mother's was. I used to stroke it as I read to her. She once put her fingers in my mouth while I tried to read. It was very funny to her; terrifying to me. What if I had slipped, bitten down, and tasted blood? She snuggled in to my shoulder and my teeth began to chatter, the words on the page swam together. Dana looked up at me, "Hey, what next? What happen next?" And her voice brought me back. I kissed the top of her head and went on with the story.

When it was finished, I saw that I'd left a drop of spittle on her hair. I touched her again to get rid of it. "Duke," she said, "Let's go 'side." I found myself wondering crazily when was the last time I went outside to play. Dana was up, dragging me by the hand. "C'mon Duke. Let's play 'side."

The little girl in the original *Frankenstein* movie—what did she say to the monster? She offered him a flower, showed him her doll; he drowned her in the pond. I wish Dana wouldn't look at me like that little girl.

✗ ✗ ✗ ✗ ✗

In the midst of the silence, in the midst of a dream, the despair and hatred of the witch who cursed me came back to me. "For all time. Forever!" she screamed as they dragged her from the room, all those years ago. Waking in our bed, I lifted Sarah's arm from across my chest, got up, got dressed, and went out in search of prey.

When I returned hours later, I knew Sarah had been up. I smelled the coffee, and the sickness. She was back in bed, asleep.

✗ ✗ ✗ ✗ ✗

My name is Manducus. These days I go by Duke. I knew Caesar, Mohammed, Buddha. I knew of Jesus of Nazareth. Something kept me from seeking him out. He was said to have the power to resurrect the dead. Could he have buried the undead?

His time passed before I could meet him. So much time has passed since my crime. It was only a whim; I was a rich man, the owner of slaves, as were all of my friends. Who would miss one slave child? Who would be shocked if the flesh of a slave child were prepared by an excellent cook to be served to distinguished guests? No one. No one but the mother of the child, a Nubian witch as it happened, who forced her way into my dining hall, screaming the curse that binds me to this day.

Of course, I didn't take the curse seriously. I believed the woman had suffered enough, but at the insistence of my guests I had her sent away. She was clearly mad. Within days I began to lose interest in my usual food. Everything seemed tasteless and dull; yet I was hungry all the time. My appetite drew me to the slave quarters, the children's filthy play area. I ordered one of the men to take a child to the kitchen. The cook would know what to do. That was the true beginning.

Word of my craving soon spread beyond the walls of my villa. Friends declined invitations. Strangers gave me hard looks in the street. Soon I had exhausted the resources of my household and the patience of the military police. I packed lightly and left home for good.

To this day I must eat the flesh of children. I must have it or I suffer the most wrenching agony—a burning convulsion of the bowels, a ferocious tightening of the skin, a swelling of the tongue, and bulging of the eyes—till my very tissues seem to choke me. Yet I cannot die, and my appetite cannot be sated.

I have traveled constantly. The discovery of my leavings is never made without oaths and blood rage. I attend the memorial services when I can. I weep with the families, for them and for myself. For while I remain at large, I am cursed beyond understanding, beyond redemption. Generation after generation, century after century, the most hated man who ever lived. The bogeyman.

✗ ✗ ✗ ✗ ✗

I was accustomed to the roar of the world—places and in between places, voices, vehicles, the elements. With Sarah came a silence that frightened me. The same sounds were there, but they now seemed indifferent or benign. My guard was down when we were together, and it was such a relief, like a hot shower after coming in from the rain. I'd catch myself humming something I'd heard on Sarah's radio and think, what have I become? And the world would raise its voice again. The hairs on the back of my neck would stand up and the damned chattering would start again. I'd rush to the nearest window or to the kitchen door. And Sarah would catch up with me, lean into me, put her arm around my waist.

"What is it, Duke? What's out there?" The roar would subside a little. I'd turn and look into her eyes. "Everything that's not us," I said.

"Phew," she smiled. "You had me worried."

It was stupid of me to have settled here. Each morning I woke with a gasp from a recurring dream of captivity and torture. We lived in a rural farmhouse. The curtains were always open and the light flooded in. The length and breadth of the world were there before me. I had forgotten that the sky had such weight. I struggled each day to collect myself, to get to the kitchen and make breakfast for my family.

My family! How unlikely, how impossible that I should have a girlfriend and a daughter after all this time. We met at the mall in the town nearby. I was passing through the area and had stopped for a bite—a terrible joke, I know. Sarah and Dana were in the parking lot, Sarah struggling to get Dana out of her car seat. I tried to suppress the chattering of my teeth as I approached to offer assistance. They rattle like castanets when I need to feed.

"C'mon, you little monster," I heard her say. Her hat came off as she lifted her daughter into her arms. She was hairless. The shock of it stopped me in my tracks. "Where's your other shoe?" she continued. "What a mess!"

"May I help?" I said. She turned toward me. Her eyes were red-rimmed and watery. Large. Her cheeks were sunken, both flushed and gray.

"Find her other shoe," she said. "Thursday's child, right?"
"What?"
"'Thursday's child has far to go.' You're a traveler."

"Yes," I said. "I've done a lot of traveling."

"I could tell," she said. "I read people fast."

I handed her the shoe. "What else can you read?"

"Put the shoe on for me."

I did. My teeth chattered violently.

"You're lonely," she said.

"It comes with traveling."

"Can you get my hat?"

I did.

"Thanks. Are you cold? Can we buy you a coffee?"

"Why not," I said.

We talked for an hour. She was youthfully confident in her insights and often wrong, but I didn't have the heart to correct her. She laughed easily in spite of her obvious illness. It was such a relief to sit and talk to someone so unaffected and so fearless. Somehow, when I was with her, the hunger subsided. I went to her house for lunch the next day—after I had taken care of my real need—and just sipped at her soup. She had made sandwiches, but Dana ate most of them. We talked through the afternoon. I played with Dana, surprised to find myself enjoying it so much, and then cooked dinner. Much later all three of us worked together on breakfast.

Sarah kept a diary. Here is an entry (it was hard for me to give up my cautious ways):

> *May 14*
>
> *It started to hurt after I ate, down low in my belly. It got so I'd only drink a coffee with lots of sugar and eat a cookie. I knew I wasn't getting proper nutrition and I needed to be here for Dana, so I got some of those liquid supplements. I'd get the vanilla and pour it in my coffee. It keeps me going. That and the support from Dana's father.*
>
> *The chemo has made my hair fall out. I'm losing weight, of course. When Duke came along I was down*

to 102 pounds. When we said goodbye after that first meeting and he shook my hand, I thought my bones would break.

Now he carries me easily between the bedroom and the kitchen. I haven't been weighed in a month, but my ribs are sticking out. My gut feels sucked in all the time, except when the pain comes. Then it writhes like something is trying to get out, not the natural way.

Duke has some money saved, so Dana eats well. He says he'll take care of her, not to worry. And I don't. She doesn't understand what's happening to me and I'm glad. But I worry about Duke. His teeth chatter in his sleep and when he's awake. I told him to see a doctor, but he says he's fine. He goes out from time to time and when he gets home, the chattering is gone. Then a week later it's back.

I hope that Dana will be okay with Duke. She will. It's only two weeks we've been together, but I love him as I never loved Dana's father. He spends so much time with both of us. He makes me feel so needed. I almost wish he didn't. I hate that I will have to leave them. I will miss my Dana growing up, becoming a woman, and having children of her own.

Sarah never knew the real me, what great evil I have done. I am thankful for that. I am a killer, but not cold-blooded. I take no pleasure in it. As much as I can, I take pains to see that my young victims do not suffer. A quick twist of the neck and they expire instantly, without pain or fear. A way in which many would choose to die, if they had a choice.

I can't remember most of my victims. There have been thousands, tens of thousands. Some stand out, of course. I suffer for every young life, but it breaks my heart to kill a child of great beauty, to know the branch will never flower, the fledgling never fly. When I can, I avoid becoming acquainted with their families.

I should have learned my lesson in the house of Beatrice di Grazza—her son Leopoldo already a musical prodigy at four, beginning to become known in Florentine society. He was receiving the best tutoring that money could buy. Mozart had written asking to meet the boy.

I was working as valet to the father, not long in the post, but easily adapting my centuries of experience to the matter of fitting in. It was a cool April morning. The boy had been left alone in the conservatory to practice. Since I would not be needed until after lunch, I was watching him from behind a pillar. He was playing a Bach aria, a slow, lovely piece. I leaned back against the wall to savor the sound. My teeth began to chatter. I groaned and clapped my hand over my mouth—too late. The music had stopped.

"Who's there?" came the young voice. "Mama, is that you?"

I stepped from the shadows. "No, young master. It is I."

"What are you doing here?"

"I came to hear you play."

"Was it good?"

"Exquisite, young master," I said. "Won't you play some more?"

He smiled and turned back to the keyboard. Before he could play a full bar, I was upon him. He died quickly. I was ravenous and the feasting was bloody. My tears diluted the gore. They scoured the countryside for months trying to find me. I longed to let them take me and put an end to my curse, but I could not bear to be locked up, to suffer the torment of being kept from my prey.

June 18
I was on a morphine IV my last time in hospital. I
needed it, God knows, but I hated it. I barely knew
when Dana and Duke were in the room. I swore at my

sister and told her to get lost when she tried to give me some of her holistic junk food.

We are alone in our home—Dana, Duke, and me. No one visits and no one calls. When Duke is away, I drag myself to the kitchen door and sit on the step. The air inside is so stale; I don't know how Duke can stand it. Sometimes I think I'll pass out from breathing my own breath over and over.

Dana loves to play in the lane, chasing grasshoppers, swinging on the tire hanging low from our tree, lying among the dandelions, looking for shapes she knows in the clouds.

It will be my last summer. I want to soak it in. So much of what Dana does is new to her: her first yellow rose, her first monarch butterfly, her first vapor trail, her first falcon. And my last. I'm a Wednesday's child. Full of woe. But I'm not feeling sorry for myself. I'm so lucky that I can see these things with her. When Duke gets home and finds me in my bed, flushed with the sun, my pillow wet with tears, I tell him I'm fine. But he can hold me, and he does.

I wanted Sarah to stay in the hospital, but it was torture being alone with Dana. I lay awake at night with the window open, drenched in sweat and shaking with the hunger, hoping another scent would distract me. During the two weeks Sarah was not with us, I had to drug little Dana so I could take her with me while I went out to find a meal. The police band radio I kept in the truck told me that I was being careless, staying here. I'd listen to a police bulletin about my activities and look down at Dana curled up beside me. How could I leave my family?

When Sarah told her doctors that she wanted to die at home, I had to suppress a yelp of relief. Somehow Sarah's presence, sick though she was, still exerted a calming influence. Perhaps it was the nearness of a natural death. Perhaps it was her love for me and my love for her. She looked at me with such innocence, with a hunger I didn't know. When she asked me if I would end her life for her, I had to leave the room. How could I tell her that her daughter's life hung in the balance, that her pain must continue for Dana to live?

The net was drawing tighter. My appetite had attracted the attention of local media. The authorities had few clues, but warnings had been issued. There is a segment of the population that knows it can't happen to them. I have always relied on their foolishness.

I began to ration myself. The lock-box in the back of my truck proved invaluable. I can keep one body—or the best parts of several, when I've had time to dress the meat—frozen for several days.

August 10

There was blood in the toilet again this morning. The pain comes and goes, but the blood keeps coming. Dr. Spiegelman said the color of the blood tells you where it comes from. Bright red comes from the lower down, black from the higher up. Mine is both red and black.

The TV is on in the front room. We like to control how much Dana watches, but lately I don't have the energy to scold her. And she is helpful to me when I need her. There is only so much you can expect from a two-year-old.

They say there's really nothing they can do for me. The cancer has spread throughout my lower body. My liver is still functioning, but they expect it to quit within the next few months. Duke bought me an auburn wig, the color I always wished I had been. He says it makes me look sexy.

I know he is much older than me. He's never told me how much. I don't know what he's afraid of—I couldn't care less. I know that he will be here for Dana after I'm gone. He loves her like his own and she loves

him. But I don't want her to see me suffer. I've asked
Duke again to help me with the end of it. It's not right
for a child to see her mother dying this way.

Sarah is gone. She begged me to release her. I couldn't refuse. Something I had done so many times; this time it tore at my heart. I longed to die with her. When I pulled the pillow away, her eyes were still open. I couldn't bear to touch them. I called the police to tell them what I had done. I also called a lawyer. I told them to hurry.

Sarah had her intuitions and she was right sometimes. She knew I had traveled, that I had known great sadness, and that I might some day have to leave. She didn't ask me to explain. It was enough for her that I would be here for Dana after she was gone and that Dana will not suffer more than she must.

I dared to lead a normal life, but how normal? Sarah was dying of cancer; Dana . . . a travesty, how could it last? I loved them both and they, incredibly, loved me.

The sirens are moaning closer. I know I will be locked away for a while. It will be agony, but my suffering will win compassion. My truck is clean and I have Sarah's diary. Her wishes are clear.

Dana will be safe from me. Tuesday's child: full of grace. She will go to her aunt. The lawyer will see that she has everything she needs. Once I am free, I will leave this area and keep moving. I was not meant to find happiness. I will not look for it again.

X X X X X

Rob Morphy is a writer, artist, and designer living in Toronto. He was born in Vancouver and grew up in Belleville, Ontario. His short story "Comes a Time" appeared in Notes Across the Aisle *(Thistledown Press, 1995) and other work has been published in a number of zines whose longevity (not to say luster) rivaled that of a rainbow.*

Rob has worked as a church caretaker, music and book seller, bartender, and union executive while struggling to do a little writing and to avoid the temptations of platform gaming and the Internet. Although his work is often horrific, this is his first attempt at a horror story. It is the story of an outcast who finds a home, for a time.

"I find I seek to die,/And seeking death, find life."
Shakespeare, *Measure for Measure.*